SUPERSTITION
Murder Club

Also by Kaine Thompson

Fiction:

FemCorps

I Remember Nobody

The Living Stones

When Gods Collide

Nonfiction:

Perilous Journey: Memoir of a Bible Smuggler

Face-to-Face: The Women Who Met Jesus

SUPERSTITION
Murder Club

A Novel by

KAINE THOMPSON

E-MAGINATIVE WRITING
Mesa, AZ

Superstition Murder Club
© 2015 by Kaine Thompson
ISBN: 978-0-9856956-4-4

Superstition Murder Club is published by:
E-maginiative Writing
Mesa, Arizona 85209

For information please direct emails to:
kaine@e-maginativewriting.com or visit our website:
www.e-maginativewriting.com

Book cover and interior design: Teri Rider, www.teririder.com

First edition, September 2015

Printed in the United States of America

10 9 8 7 6 5 4 3 2   16 17 18 19 20 21 22 23

Dedicated to the ladies
of the water aerobics class
at Monte Vista Village Resort
who encouraged me to write this book
and provided the inspiration.

LIST OF SUPERSTITION MURDER CLUB MEMBERS

(First Name Alphabetical)

"BABE" (BRUNA) WINTERS, 80, German refugee, leader of Superstition Aquatics Club

BELLA ADLER, 85, widow, dresses with flair, retired advertising executive

"BOOM BOOM" KLUTTERBUCK, 87, retired pole dancer, loves cats, wine and men

CICIE KIMBRO, 89, retired drama teacher, leader of the new Superstition Murder Club

"DIDDI" (DORTHEA) BLUM, 95, never married, sophisticated, protective of her privacy

JOSIE SIMONE, 72, married, quiet, shy, passionate, had an affair with the victim

LORETTA DUKES, 70, married, attractive, Christian, spiritual leader of the ladies

MADDIE INGERSOLL, 85, widow, mother of 10, son is a deputy district attorney

MADGE ZIEGLER, 84, German refugee, devout Christian, suffers from a bad back

MARGARITA BROWN, 75, Filipina beauty, recently widowed, loves to dance

MIMI BRADSHAW, 68, a redheaded widow, former schoolteacher with a hidden past

SANDRA FLEMING, 70, married, former newspaper reporter, known as "Miss Behavin"

"SWEETS" (JOSELYN) SWEETS, 70s, married, rides a Harley and plays the organ

VERONICA MOON, 60, spends her time at the pool working on her tan

CHAPTER ONE

Alice Sheridan woke from a bad dream—black wings rising up in front of her and she couldn't get away. She blinked and waited for her eyes to catch up to her agitated brain. She focused on the clock until she could see the hands clearly. It was five in the morning. She got out of bed, threaded her thin arms through the sleeves of her housecoat, found her slippers and shuffled into the kitchen. She had a feeling that something unpleasant was waiting for her.

She scanned the counters until her eyes rested on her broken coffeemaker. That was it! Coffee! She selected her favorite mug from the cupboard, opened the front door and wandered down the middle of the street.

The Arizona sky was a dusky purple, a precursor to daybreak. A warm breeze ruffled her short white hair. She stepped up a curb and shambled carefully along the shadowed walkway. As she neared her turn-off, a cottontail darted in front of her, making her stumble and nearly lose her balance. She hurried her steps, watching the path for more rabbits. At a metal meshed gate, she stretched her arm to full extension and pulled down on the handle to enter the pool area.

The orange, red and purple umbrellas were open. Vacant lounge chairs were strategically arranged for the swimmers and sun-worshippers that would soon fill the space. The shimmering blue water of the main pool reflected the growing light of day. As Alice gazed at the water all thoughts left her mind. She was hypnotized by its stillness, its beckoning blue. Suddenly, she became aware of a presence rising up behind her. She turned in time to see a large black bat rush past, its wings unfurled.

"Oh!"

Her heart thudded in her shrunken chest and her bowels clenched. What was that? Where was she? What was she doing here? She looked at the mug in her hand and it reassured and reminded her that she was on a mission. Coffee!

She scurried along the sidewalk to what she hoped would be the way out. She miscalculated and arrived at the lower pool. Someone had left something large in the pool and it marred the beauty of the quiet water. The sight unnerved her. She scanned the walls that enclosed the pool area, trying to get her bearings. She had a momentary attack of panic until she realized where she was. There! The coffee bar was just on the other side of the wall.

She scampered around the outer edge of the pool and found another unlocked gate. Standing on tiptoe she pulled down on the handle and pushed through.

With a sigh of relief she found the coffee bar that was always available for the residents of Superstition Way Resort. She filled her cup from an enormous urn and mixed in a hefty amount sugar. She selected a table, sat in a cushioned chair and sipped appreciatively while she waited for daylight. This was her favorite time of the day.

Within a few minutes, Gary Smith, a resort maintenance man walked by, dressed in his usual khaki shirt and shorts and greeted her.

"Morning, Mrs. Sheridan. I see you've got your coffee."

"Gary, I have a bone to pick with you!"

This was not her usual response, so Gary stopped and walked up to her. He had a special tender feeling for this 90-year-old waif.

"What's the trouble, ma'am?"

"It's not right for you to leave a body in the pool."

"Excuse me?"

"The body. In the pool. Someone needs to take it out before it fouls the water! I don't swim myself, but the ones who do won't like it at all!"

Chapter Two

The Superstition Mountains rose from the valley floor like an aging battleship, purple gray with fissures of rust: chipped, broken, ancient, but still dangerous. Many a prospector had lost his life scouring the Superstitions in a vain attempt to find the elusive Lost Dutchman Mine and its fabled mother lode of gold. If the hapless miners had consulted members of the local Yavapai/Apache Nation, they would have learned that they were more likely to find the entrance to hell or, at the very least, the origins of the hot, volatile winds that created the periodic dust storms.

However, this superstition did not deter the snowbirds that came from all over the country and the provinces of Canada to escape the ice and snow during the winter months. Superstition Way Resort, a retirement community located in Peralta Canyon, southeast of Phoenix, was their haven, a respite from the cold, a place to relax and enjoy life in a safe cocoon of bucolic ease. Besides hot, sunny, cloudless days, the resort offered an array of amenities, including two pools and spa, library, multi-media room, arts and crafts room, billiard room, card rooms, lapidary, silversmith shop, ceramics and woodworking shops, and fitness centers. Residents could also enjoy a putting green and driving range, croquet, lawn bowling, softball, shuffleboard, tennis and pickleball. During the high season, November to March, 1800 snowbirds called it home, resulting in a sudden and frenetic pace of activity, congestion and lifelong friendships. Once they flew back home to the north, the remaining 200 residents sighed with relief at the slower pace, including eighty-year-old Babe Winters, the leader of the Superstition Aquatics Club.

At quarter to seven on that hot August morning, Babe was the first to arrive at the pool house. She was a petite woman wearing a pink terrycloth shift over her bathing suit, a towel draped over her arm and a cloth cap on her silver hair. She didn't know what to make of the police car and ambulance parked in front. Suddenly, red lights flashed and the ambulance backed up and sped away. She frowned and bit her lip, staring at the police car.

Just then, Madge Ziegler rode up on her three-wheel bike and Boom Boom Klutterbuck, 87, skidded to a halt in her golf cart.

"What's happening?" Madge asked, groaning in pain as she got off her bike.

"Whatever it is, it better not interfere with our class," Babe announced to her friends as they approached.

As a World War II refugee from Germany, Babe had learned stamina and discipline. She was the perfect leader of the club because she was sweet and soft on the outside but iron on the inside. She kept a firm grip on club attention and attendance. As she frequently told her members, it takes discipline to get up every morning and exercise, but if they wanted to live long healthy lives, they had better show up and be ready to work out. She may have been only 4'11", but the ladies didn't dare cross her.

"Anyone we know?" Boom Boom asked, watching the ambulance turn a corner and disappear.

"Must be bad. Police are here," Babe reported gloomily in her accented English.

"Who's that in the back seat?" Madge asked, shading her eyes with her hand, scrutinizing the police car. A bright red visor covered her short white hair. Also a refugee from Germany, Madge was 84, tall, with a pronounced stoop. She had been widowed early in life and was childless. She suffered from chronic back problems, but her faith in God, sharp mind and willingness to help anyone made her popular among her peers.

The three ladies inched forward until they could make out the hunched figure in the back seat of the police car.

"Oh, my gosh! It's Alice!" Madge gasped.

"Give me an ever-living break!" Boom Boom huffed. "Never thought they'd call the cops on her just because she wanders off. I'm going to get to the bottom of this."

Boom Boom was a dynamo wrapped in a small

package with an endless supply of jokes and stories. She often leaped before she looked, but her heart was always in the right place. At 87, she had yet to discover old age.

"Now don't insert yourself where you don't belong," Madge cautioned, but Boom Boom was already knocking on the window, trying to get Alice to roll it down.

"I'm going to set up for class," Babe stated. "It's got nothing to do with us and the others will be arriving soon."

As Babe left, Madge stood helplessly by as Boom Boom opened the back door of the patrol car. Having hid from German *polizei* as a child, she believed that nothing good ever came from interfering with the police, but her curiosity got the better of her and she moved closer in time to hear Alice answering Boom Boom's question.

"I didn't kill him," Alice whined. "The bat did. I just wanted coffee."

"What did she say?" Madge asked.

"She said she didn't kill him; the bat did."

"Kill who?"

"How should I know? Stop talking and I'll find out."

"Who's dead, Alice?"

Before Alice could answer, Bella Adler roared up in her car and parked right next to the police car, nearly hitting Madge who flattened herself against the side panel of the police car. Boom Boom jumped into the back seat with Alice and pulled the door shut. Bella slammed on the brake. She rolled down the window.

"What's going on? Who's that?"

"You nearly hit us!" Madge cried, wiping the dust from her backside.

"Holy crap, Bella!" Boom Boom swore, stepping out onto the street. "It's Alice."

"Sorry, girls, I got distracted by the police car. Alice! What're you doing in there? Get out here this instant!" Bella commanded.

Bella, 85, was a forceful personality with great style. She was known for her generosity and kindness, but had a bit of the devil in her. She wore a red and white striped sundress with a matching hat. Her lips were outlined in bright red lipstick, which perfectly matched her fingernails and toenails.

She quickly took matters into her own hands and had Alice out of the back seat of the police car and into her front seat within minutes. Alice helplessly grabbed onto her arm and started to cry.

"I'm taking her home. She's in a terrible state!"

"She said she didn't kill him," Boom Boom informed her.

"What? Pshaw! Look at her. Absurd."

Boom Boom gave Alice's thin arm a squeeze and

Madge patted her back. Alice looked up and smiled like a child.

"Dead. Like a starfish," she said quite clearly. "Dead. Dead. Dead." Then she whined, "I want to go home. Where's Jeffrey? I want Jeffrey."

"Great. She wants her dead husband. I'll put her to bed and be back in a jiffy," Bella asserted. "Don't let Babe start class without me. Promise."

"Okay," Madge said reluctantly, shutting the car door.

"Let's see what's going on," Boom Boom urged, grabbing Madge's arm.

As Bella tore down the street, Boom Boom and Madge started toward the pool house. They were just about to enter when the rest of the ladies from the Superstition Aquatics Club appeared from different directions in their golf carts, on bikes or on foot. There was Cicie Kimbro, Maddie Ingersoll, Diddi Blum, Josie Simone, Joselyn Sweets, known as Sweets; Margarita Brown, Veronica Moon, Mimi Bradshaw, Sandra Fleming and Loretta Dukes.

They were startled by the presence of the police car and went en masse to find out what was happening inside. They entered the alcove to the dressing rooms that led out to the pool and were dumbfounded to see Babe standing at the gate with the boom box still in her hand.

"We can't go in," Babe complained as the ladies joined her.

"What do you mean we can't go in," Sandra fumed. "I can!"

As a former reporter with the *San Jose Courier*, Sandra was used to going where she didn't belong. Now in her early seventies, she didn't exactly break the rules, but she gleefully bent them whenever she could.

She opened the gate and pushed through. The ladies as one surged behind her, too late realizing that they had broken through a yellow police tape barrier. Maddie got tangled up in it and Josie stopped to help her remove it from her feet. They hurried to follow their friends who were circling the pool.

"Hey, hey, hey! You can't come in here," a young policeman shouted, coming towards them with his arms outstretched as if he were going to corral them like a flock of birds.

The ladies, with an average age of eighty, were wily and limber. They scattered, forcing the policeman to circle and chase them in a most unprofessional manner. When he caught Diddi Blum by the arm, he didn't know what to do with her.

"Young man," she said, in her haughtiest tone, "I'm ninety-five years old and no one has ever laid a hand on me and lived to tell about it! Let me go!"

The police officer let go of her arm as if he had

been burned. He backed away and changed direction. Diddi sank into a chair at one of the tables and wiped her face with a towel.

Boom Boom, a former pole dancer in an exotic club who had retired after her second hip replacement, was able to circumvent the young officer's efforts and make it to the lower pool where all the action was taking place. Loretta, Sandra, Margarita and Mimi quickly out maneuvered him and circled to the left toward the lower pool. Boom Boom completely escaped him by switching directions and going to the right.

The rest of the ladies sat down with Diddi at the table. Madge quickly filled them in on what Alice had said.

"Killed! Did she really say killed?" Sweets interrupted. Although in her late seventies, Sweets was in great shape and only her white hair gave away her age. She was a former Army field nurse, and when she wasn't riding her Harley, she was at home, playing her Lowrey Deluxe organ, much to her husband's delight. She had learned to play at least fifty tunes, including his favorite, *Proud Mary.*

"Alice killed someone?" Seventy-two-year-old Josie asked, choking on the word.

"No, she saw someone who was killed."

"Alice can't remember anything any more," Babe reassured them. "I'm sure there's nothing to it."

"I don't know, Babe. Something happened or there wouldn't be police," Cicie argued. At 90, Cicie was sharp as a tack and had the ability to see the big picture. In her youth, she had been in off Broadway productions and later taught high school drama. She still sang and danced in the resort theater's *Spring Follies*. She had great insight into people's motivation. "Somebody must have drowned," she insisted.

"She said killed." Madge repeated, determinedly. "There's been a murder!"

"Murder!" Maddie gasped. "Maybe we should go! We don't want to get mixed up in any murder." Maddie, 84, was the mother of the group, always looking out for people's welfare. She wasn't the oldest, but as a mother of ten children, her maternal instincts had never switched off.

"I don't care! It's after seven. We're running late! I'm setting up the CD," Babe announced.

"You're not going to have class now, are you?" Josie asked, shocked. Josie was a Midwest gal, the epitome of kindness and gentility. She and her husband had left Iowa behind and become permanent residents two years earlier. She was a pretty woman who appreciated the finer things of life. She loved travel, fine wine, good clothes and more than anything else, adventure. She had been eager to show off her new magenta swimsuit, but now it didn't seem appropriate. Someone was dead.

"You know our rules," Babe countered, seeing rebellion in the ranks. "What are they?"

"Neither cold, nor wind, nor blazing sun will keep us from our aquatics fun," the ladies repeated together.

With that, Babe plugged in the boom box and inserted the CD. The ladies rose and began removing their robes and shifts.

"Wait a minute," Madge asserted. "We can't start yet. I promised Bella we'd wait for her. She took Alice home."

"And the other girls went down to the lower pool," Sweets reminded Babe. "We'll wait for them," she said, daring to disagree.

Babe wasn't happy, but under the circumstances, she allowed them to persuade her to wait before starting the class.

"I'll wait five more minutes. But tomorrow," she commanded, "we start on time!"

CHAPTER THREE

Chief of Detectives Magnus Varland, whose recent sixtieth birthday had filled him with horror, was even more horrified to see five old ladies in bathing suits circling his crime scene and heading his way. Four were approaching from the left, and one from the right; a tiny grey-haired biddy, wearing a black and white swimsuit covered by a gauzy wrap, fluttering around her. She strode toward him with a pronounced limp that did nothing to slow her down or lessen her determination to question him.

"Hey there! Are you in charge?" she shouted, waving her hand to get his attention. "You there! What's going on? Can we help?"

At 6'3" Detective Varland was an imposing man, broad-shouldered and muscular. His sandy hair, receding at the hairline, hung limply above his ears and neckline. His near perfect oval face had refined cheekbones and indentations on either side of a slightly crooked nose. He sprouted puffy bags under light brown eyes, cultivated by long, sleepless nights and poor diet, which somewhat marred his good looks. He was wearing a light gray, rumpled suit with a blue tie, slightly askew.

He ground his teeth on the answer he would have given any other "helpful citizen" who was contaminating his crime scene. The EMTs had just removed the body. He was fairly certain someone had moved it before he got there. He had already questioned Bart Ferguson, the resort's security officer who had called 911. He seemed like a responsible man, a retired Marine in his eighties, who had assured him that he had not touched the body and had found the victim lying face-up on the concrete beside the lower pool.

Varland gave a meaningful nod to a police officer that he noticed was trying hard not to smile. The officer stepped forward, but was unsure of what the detective wanted him to do with the women coming towards them. Varland wasn't sure himself.

He cleared his throat and softened his answer as she came within earshot, "No thank you, ma'am. We've got things well under control. I'd appreciate it if you would follow Officer Dennison back behind the crime scene tape."

She plainly ignored him as her four friends joined her.

"So, who is it, Boom Boom?" asked the dark-haired woman in a purple suit.

"Did you find out anything?" asked the redhead.

"Nothing yet. I was just about to ask Officer . . ." Boom Boom turned and faced him with a quizzical look on her face.

"Chief of Detectives Magnus Varland, PCPD," he

flashed the shield on his belt and answered right away, as if his mother had asked him where he had been all night. "I'm sorry, ma'am, but I'm going to have to ask you and your friends to leave. You may not have realized it but this is a crime scene and there's an active investigation in progress."

"Well, we kind of got that from the police tape," the tiny old woman giggled.

"I told you it was murder, Loretta!" screeched a blond dressed in a blue bathing suit, pointing at a woman in a hot pink swimsuit. "I've got a nose for crime." She was compactly built and formidable. Her narrowed blue eyes and combative stance looked like trouble to Detective Varland.

"Was it one of ours?" Loretta, the lady in the hot pink suit, asked him, looking pale and concerned. She was attractive and slender with blond highlights in her short hair. She must be at least seventy, but filled out her suit well--too well. Detective Varland had to avert his gaze. In his twenty-six years on the force, he had never been surrounded by five inquisitive women in swimsuits, old enough to be his mother if not his grandmother.

"Was someone murdered, Chief Varland?" Boom Boom asked.

"This is a crime scene, ladies," he replied with great officiousness, trying to reassert himself, "and anyone crossing my police line is subject to arrest."

"We've never had a murder here. Lots of people die, but nobody kills them," offered the redhead, sporting large round sunglasses and dressed in a bright yellow tie-dyed poncho. She was tall, but shielded by a dark-haired woman in a purple suit.

"What happened?" the blond in the blue suit demanded.

"Chief?" The woman they called Boom Boom shook his sleeve with her tiny hand. "Can you tell us who it was? We know practically everyone in the resort, and those we don't know we know about."

"That's right," the redhead agreed. "We know where all the bodies are buried."

"Oh Mimi!" the blond woman in blue shrieked with laughter. "I can't believe you said that! Too funny!"

"It isn't funny, Sandra. Someone died!"

"You're right, Margarita," she agreed, chagrined. "It just struck me funny, that's all. Bodies buried. Only he wasn't buried was he."

"Alice said he was in the pool. Like a starfish she said," Boom Boom added. "He must have drowned."

"That makes no sense! If it were an accident, it wouldn't be a crime scene! It's murder, I'm telling you! I worked the crime beat for the *Courier*, remember."

The ladies began talking all at once until Detective Varland realized that he had again lost control.

"Ladies. Ladies! Now listen to me. I've been nice,

but I am ordering you to leave. Please follow Officer Dennison out of the area."

"Are you going to arrest us, Chief Varland?" Boom Boom asked in a sultry voice, leaning into him, patting his sleeve with her bony hand. "Are you going to put the handcuffs on me or will it be that cute young man?"

Detective Magnus Varland was speechless. The young police officer barked a laugh, but quickly recovered and stood at attention.

"Boom Boom leave the poor man alone," Loretta said. "He's just doing his job."

"I'm only teasing him," Boom Boom replied coolly.

"How long?" demanded the blond. "How long will the pool be off limits to us?"

"Until we're done with it," Detective Varland snarled, growing impatient. He rose to his full height, narrowed his eyes and clenched his jaw, which usually put the fear of God into people. It had no effect on the ladies.

"You mean we can't swim here until you figure out who killed the guy?" Sandra fumed. "Total bummer! Can you believe that?"

"Babe will have a stroke," the woman called Mimi said.

"At least tell us his name. We're sure to know him. Maybe we can speed up your investigation," Loretta offered.

"I can't say this any stronger, ladies. I definitely do not want your help with my investigation. I want all of you to leave. Immediately!"

"I'm waiting for my handcuffs, Chief," Boom Boom cooed, tapping his chest.

He stepped back. "Officer Dennison, please escort these nice ladies out of the pool area and get their names and addresses before they leave."

Just at that moment, the sound of an exercise routine emitted from the upper pool.

"What is that?" Detective Varland asked, whirling around. "What's that sound?"

"That's our exercise music," Boom Boom replied. "Babe always starts at seven. Guess we're running late today."

"Are you telling me there are more of you and they're in the upper pool?"

"Oh yes, Chief. Lots. We never miss a class. Babe would tan our hides. I don't know what she's going to do when she hears you're going to close down the pool."

"Isn't she friends with the county supervisor?" the redheaded woman Mimi asked. "Wasn't her husband his lawyer?"

"That's right. They used to play golf together," Sandra smirked.

"Officer Dennison, stop them! That's an order!"

The young officer ran around the side of the

lower pool and up the sidewalk to the main pool. He was gone for some time, but the sound from the CD continued.

Detective Varland felt his sleeve being jerked again. He looked down at the sweet wrinkled face that reminded him of his fourth grade teacher. "I can get them to leave if you answer my questions," Boom Boom offered.

He sighed, "Go ahead, ma'am."

"Who was he?"

"Don't know. No ID. We'll have to wait for fingerprints."

"Resident here?"

"Don't know that either."

"How'd he die?"

"Most likely drowned. It's not that unusual. We investigate any unnatural death--and that's all you get. Now, will you please tell your friends to leave my crime scene?"

"You got it, Chief. I'm in Unit #1305 if you want to chat sometime. I've got a nice Merlot I'd love to share with you. Come on, girls."

Boom Boom led the way and the other ladies reluctantly followed her up to the main pool. Within a few minutes, the sound from the boom box ended.

Detective Varland gave a sigh of relief and re-examined the perimeter of the lower pool. He took his time, hoping to find something the officers and the medical investigators might have missed. No such luck. There was nothing more for him to gain.

He strolled up to the upper pool to find it empty, except for the two officers. True to her word Boom Boom had moved the ladies to another location. Officer Dennison was restoring the police tape.

On the surface, it appeared that the victim had fallen into the lower pool in the early hours of the morning and drowned. Varland would have called it an accidental drowning, if not for the fact that the side of his skull had been crushed by something hard, wielded by someone with intent to kill. No murder weapon had been found so the killer must have taken it with him. The victim was wearing only boxer shorts. His clothes had not been found. He would have to wait for his Crime Scene Unit, also known as the CSU, and the autopsy reports from the Forensics Lab in Phoenix before he could identify the victim.

Officer McLaren was approaching quickly, wiping his forehead with his sleeve.

"Did you get their names?" Varland asked.

"Yes, sir, but . . ."

"Good job, McClaren. That was certainly a first for me."

"Yes, sir. I'm sorry, sir, but our witness is gone."

"The old lady who found the body? I wouldn't have thought she could walk, much less elude you."

"Yes, sir. I know, sir, but when I got back to the

car, she was gone. She's so old and feeble I didn't think she was going anywhere. She seemed to like sitting in the car."

"That's alright, McClaren. You got her name and house number, right?"

"Oh, yes, sir!"

"Then I'll pay her a visit. You and Officer Dennison go back to the station and write up your reports. I'll check in with you later."

It took less than a minute for Detective Varland to drive up to Alice Sheridan's house. It was a beige doublewide mobile home on an established lot. It looked a little worse for wear. He opened the grillwork door and knocked on the inner door. No one answered. He knocked again. The door opened.

Boom Boom grabbed his hand and pulled him inside.

CHAPTER FOUR

The ladies from the Superstition Aquatics Club were arranged around the living room and kitchen area, sipping tea, and openly staring at the detective. They were no longer in their swimsuits but dressed in summer clothes.

Bella Adler approached him with a plate of sweet rolls. "I'm Bella, Detective Varland. I hope you'll forgive me. I brought Alice home. She's asleep now, but I expect her to wake up shortly. Please sit and have a sweet roll while you wait."

She pushed the plate into his hand and guided him by the elbow to the dining table. The ladies at the table moved their chairs to accommodate the detective.

"Get him a fork, Sandra," Bella directed. "Would you like a cup of tea? I'm afraid that's all we have to offer. Alice's coffeemaker is broken."

"Cream and sugar?" Madge asked.

"Okay," he muttered.

Bella quickly poured him a cup from a cracked teapot. Sandra thrust a fork into his hand, and by the look she gave him, he automatically took a bite of the sweet roll. She sat next to him.

"Mmm," he said, trying to smile, nodding his head at her.

"Is that nice young man with you?" Boom Boom asked, scooting closer and plucking at his sleeve.

"No, just me." He nibbled on his roll, surveying the room full of women. They were all looking at him.

Sandra, the retired reporter, was bursting with questions and opened her mouth, but one look from Bella and she closed it and sat back. Sweets sat opposite the detective, giving him an appraising look as if she were trying to assess whether he was up to the job.

Next to her sat Mimi, her red hair gleaming from the sun coming in through the kitchen curtains revealing her startling green eyes. Her intense gaze was directed toward the detective. She appeared nervous. Her lips twitched and she swallowed often.

Madge, leaning against the wall, was frowning. Her entire spirit was unsettled by the victim's death. She did the only thing she could do; pray under her breath. She felt as if she shouldn't be there, but she wasn't about to be left out.

It was the same for the rest of the ladies. When they couldn't have their class, they had agreed to check on Bella at Alice's house. It wasn't strange that they went together. Their usual routine was to gather after class for coffee and eat whatever treats someone brought. It was a way for them to keep up on resort news and keep tabs on one another.

What was strange was that no one was talking. The room was absolutely quiet. Before the detective had arrived, it had literally hummed with their speculations on what had occurred at the pool.

Now everyone was watching the detective eat his cake. He appeared to be having trouble swallowing.

"Did you get him some tea?" Maddie asked.

"Of course I did," Sandra barked. "More tea, Detective Varland?"

He tried to speak but nothing came out. He cleared his throat. "Ahm, no. I'm fine, thank you. Would someone check on Mrs. Sheridan and see if she shows signs of waking. I need to speak with her as soon as possible. It will be either here or later down at the station. I'd prefer to do it here."

"I'll check." Mimi said and ran out of the room. She moved so fast her red hair and brilliant yellow sundress were a blur.

"Maybe we should wake her up?" Josie wondered. "I don't think she could handle going to the police station alone."

"I can take her," Loretta stated. "Only I agree with Josie. She shouldn't go. It might be too much stress for her."

Loretta had a calming effect on the ladies. Raised in West Virginia as a coal miner's daughter, she had suffered great deprivation as a child. She ran away from home when she was sixteen and her education had suffered, which still caused her great embarrassment. She converted to Christianity in her twenties and was a devout follower. She married well and wanted for nothing. She was a humble, caring woman, never pushing her beliefs on others; however, she was the one everyone went to when they were going through troubles.

"We should wake her up," Diddi said, matter-of-factly. "It's best. She may know something. At least we'll be here if she needs us."

Ninety-five-year-old Diddi didn't speak often, but when she did everyone paid attention. She was extremely independent and protective of her past. She had lived a long life, but nothing much was known about her, other than that she liked martinis, had travelled extensively in her youth, had never married and had enough money to live at the resort.

"I'll go!" Sandra volunteered as she stood up. Sweets got up and barred her way.

"Bella should go," she insisted. "She put her to bed."

"That's right," Diddi agreed. "Bella should do it."

The ladies nodded their ascent and Bella got up. Sandra frowned and sat down, crossing her arms. Detective Varland set his empty plate on the table and stood up in order to follow. At that moment his cell phone rang.

"Excuse me a minute," he said to no one in particular. He opened the front door and went out.

All eyes turned back to Maddie. There was only a second of silence before someone spoke.

"So, go on, Maddie. You were about to tell us what Gary said," Veronica urged excitedly.

As the youngest at sixty, Veronica was indulged and pampered. The ladies cherished her long blond hair, plump body and vitality, the fading vestiges of youth. They listened to her when she had something to say, and they appreciated that she, in turn, listened to them when they were talking. She had an Internet business selling purified water systems, but spent most of her time at the pool, reading and working on her tan.

"Maddie!" Sandra snapped.

"What?"

"Gary said . . ."

"Oh, right. Gary. Well, you know I couldn't find my shoes, so I left after the rest of you," Maddie whispered. "I found them under the table. I usually leave them in the dressing room . . ."

"Never mind that, Maddie," Josie said, exasperated.

"Speak up!" Cicie shouted. Several of the ladies nodded their heads.

Maddie scooted forward on the couch and increased her volume. "He was spraying ant killer by the men's dressing room. You know the ants are real bad this year. Almost as bad as the mice. I don't like putting poison out because of the dogs. If any of them ate it I would never forgive . . . what was I saying? Sorry, I got side tracked, oh yes; so while I was talking to Gary about the ants, I asked him if he knew about the murder. You'll never guess what he said!" She took a big pause for effect.

"What?" they all shouted.

"He's the one who fished him out. The dead man! With that hooky thing."

"Poor Gary!" Josie exclaimed. "How horrible."

"And you're not going to believe this! He was in his underwear."

"Boxers or briefs?" Boom Boom asked, punching Sweets in the arm, suppressing a giggle.

"Gary or the stiff?" Sweets responded, punching her back, openly grinning.

"I don't know," Maddie said, searching her memory. "He never told me which kind."

"Who was it?" Madge asked, leaning against the door, with her arms crossed. "We need to pray for his family."

Everyone leaned forward to catch what Maddie was going to say.

Maddie scrunched up her forehead. She brightened a moment, frowned, and then shook her head. "I can't remember."

"Nooo, Maddie. Try to remember," Veronica urged.

"You can do it," Sweets said. "Think!"

"You can't have forgotten," Sandra fumed. "It's less than an hour ago!"

"Don't rush her, Sandra" Cicie said. "Give her space. It'll come to her. Don't worry about it, Maddie. You'll remember."

"Let's talk about something else," Babe suggested. "I want everyone to be at the pool on time tomorrow."

There was dead silence as the ladies looked at each other. Babe looked from one to the other and could tell something was up.

"What?" she asked. "Tell me!"

No one spoke.

"There isn't going to be a class tomorrow, or the next day, or the next," Cicie said sadly. "It's closed until they solve the case!"

"Who said?" Babe challenged, her face going pale.

"Him. The Chief," Boom Boom confirmed sadly, pointing to the door.

"You know what that means?" Babe stated, standing to her feet.

"What?" the ladies asked, looking to their leader.

"It means we're going to have to solve the case to get back into the pool!"

The ladies began talking all at once. The thought of getting involved in a murder investigation thrilled some and terrified others.

"We could call ourselves the Superstition Murder Club," Veronica announced.

"Oh, that's splendid!" Cicie nodded. The other ladies also nodded.

"We are not changing our name!" Babe stated defensively.

"Bennie! Bennie Uzul," Maddie shouted, smiling broadly, waving her hands. "That's who! Oh, poor Bennie. Poor, poor man."

"You did it! Good for you, Maddie!" Cicie cried, getting up and hugging her.

"Who?" Veronica asked. "I never heard of him. Is he from here? Anyone know him?"

The ladies all looked down at their laps, at the ceiling, or at each other, but no one offered any information.

"No one?" Veronica was stunned. In her short time with the Superstition Aquatics Club she had learned that very little went on at the resort that one of the ladies didn't know about. She looked at each one of them. She turned to Sandra who was one of the best sources for information because she used to work in the resort's front office and was a former reporter. She had great interviewing skills and often people told her things without realizing she was filing it away in her well-ordered brain.

"What about you, Miss Behavin?" Veronica cajoled, using Sandra's pet name.

Sandra's face was red and she looked as if she had swallowed a lemon. It was a shock to see. Rarely was she at a loss for words. Everyone stopped talking.

"You know something," Margarita challenged. "I can see it in your eyes."

"You can see it in her whole body," Diddi cackled.

"Tell us, Sandra," Madge urged. "What do you know about Bennie Uzul?"

"I need to talk to my husband," was all she said before she opened the door, moving Madge out of the way, and darted out of the house.

The ladies broke out in a flurry of conversation, each trying to figure out what Sandra's bizarre action meant. Just then, Madge cried out. She had been leaning against the door when it was pushed open. She moved quickly to the other side of the room, rubbing her back.

Detective Varland entered and the women fell silent once again. They all stared at him with the same expectant look. He cleared his throat.

"Who was that who just left? She seemed to be in a hurry."

"That was Sandra Fleming. She had to talk to her husband," Cicie said.

"I have identification of the victim," the detective growled. "Benito Uzul. He lived in the next resort over, Costa del Grande. Anyone know him?" He looked around the room and saw blank faces gazing back at him. "Well, if you hear anything, please let me know. I'll leave my cards here."

He tossed a few business cards on the table and went

down the hallway to Alice's bedroom. Within a few seconds, Bella and Mimi rushed into the living room.

"He kicked us out," Mimi explained to their questioning looks.

"She looked so scared, but he wouldn't let us stay," Bella added. "I'll be surprised if he gets anything out of her. Poor dear, she just isn't with it anymore."

"It was Bennie Uzul, Bella" Maddie whispered loudly.

"Bennie!"

"What? Who?" Mimi asked, stumbling over one of the kitchen chairs. She quickly sat down. Diddi went to the couch and sat next to Maddie, grabbing her hand and whispering reassurance to her. Loretta scooted over so Bella could sit down.

"He is, I mean was, Bennie Uzul," Maddie said again. "Only the detective called him Benito. I don't know why he called him that, but it was our Bennie, Diddi."

"You've said enough, Maddie," Diddi shushed her.

"Sandra knows something, too, but she's not talking," Sweets said. "She went out of here like the devil was chasing her."

"I can't believe the ladies of the Superstition Aquatics Club don't know him," Veronica laughed. "I think that's a first. Is it because he's from Casa del Grande?"

Her laughter caught in her throat as she saw the guilty expressions on everyone's faces. Was it a conspiracy? These women were always willing to share what they knew about the people they knew, but here they were clamped down tighter than a prescription bottle lid.

"You guys know something. What's going on?"

"Look, I've got some thinking to do," Bella said, "and I'm not ready to say anything, but if anyone wants to meet at my house at one, I'll have plenty of drinks available and those who want can put their cards on the table. Got it?"

The ladies acknowledged Bella's proposition with varying degrees of acceptance. Babe took that moment to stand up and move to where everyone could see and hear her.

"That's enough for now. I declare this meeting of the Superstition Aquatics Club adjourned!"

With that, she opened the door and hobbled out.

When Detective Varland returned to the living room, no one was there. At first, he chastised himself for not getting statements from them, but then he had a sinking feeing that he would probably see them again. He should be so unlucky!

His interview with Alice Sheridan had been routine and a waste of time. She didn't know anything. She didn't even know who she was, let alone the victim. He had left her happily watching television from her bed, the control clasped in her claw-like hands. He pulled out his cell phone and dialed a number.

"Hi, Vana. It's me. I'm at the home of Mrs. Alice Sheridan at Superstition Way Resort off Chandler Street, Unit #1207. I need someone to contact her family and let them know she needs greater care and that she's a witness in a murder investigation. No, I don't have the number. That's why I'm calling you. Just take care of it. Patch me over to Officer McClaren.

"McClaren, did you finish writing up the statement from that security guard? Great. I'm coming back. Put it on my desk. Are the techies from CSU finished? Okay. I'll give Clement a call. Thanks."

He hung up and looked around the room, chuckling as he thought of the sweet little dears he'd encountered. He admired their spunk and their eagerness to help. Poor things. It must be quite boring for them living so far from the action. A murder was probably like a shot of adrenaline to them. They probably hadn't had this much excitement in their entire lives.

He noticed all his business cards were gone, and then he spied the tray of mini-sweet rolls on the table. When he left the home of Alice Sheridan, his suit coat pockets were bulging.

CHAPTER FIVE

Only seven ladies showed up at Bella's house that afternoon. Diddi had a hair appointment. Loretta had to fix dinner for her husband. Maddie didn't approve of drinking and Babe had developed a headache. Josie said she would try to make it, but hadn't arrived. Madge's back was acting up and she made Boom Boom promise to call her once they had heard what Sandra had to say.

That left Veronica, Cicie, Mimi, Bella, Boom Boom, Sweets, Margarita and Sandra, whom Bella had called and specifically invited.

Bella's home was one of the show places in the resort. Before she had retired, she had been a design executive at one of the biggest advertising agencies in San Francisco. Her ability to decorate and create perfect settings was unmatched. Her home was comfortable, with perfect lighting and a rich well-appointed decor.

As the ladies arrived, the first thing she did was take their drink order. She bustled about her well stocked bar set on a highly polished sideboard. The women admired her living room and made themselves at home. Sandra couldn't sit. She paced back and forth. Cicie elbowed Veronica as they observed Sandra's growing agitation.

"Hey, Miss Behavin', why don't you sit down and relax," Mimi prodded.

"Yeah, you're wearing a groove in the parquet," Boom Boom joked.

"Leave me alone," Sandra replied, frowning. "I gotta think."

Bella pushed a tea trolley into the center of the living room, forcing Sandra to sit. On its mirrored surface were two Manhattans, two glasses of Merlot, a vodka martini and three margaritas. She also included a plate of sliced cheeses and crackers. Everyone took a libation and scooped up snacks. Sandra snatched her margarita and downed it.

Bella retrieved a pitcher and refilled Sandra's glass. Sandra, her face flushed with embarrassment, thanked her and sipped more slowly.

"I think I should tell you, girls, that Alice's family arrived this afternoon," Bella stated, looking solemn.

"You mean . . ." Boom Boom asked, her eyes filled with horror.

"I'm afraid so."

No one said anything, but concentrated on their drinks. The thought of Alice's fate weighed heavily on them. Every once in awhile, they looked up and glanced at Sandra. She appeared more composed, but not ready to talk. She had that set to her jaw they all knew well. Her lips were compressed into a straight line. To ease the strained awkwardness, Cicie stood up and faced her friends.

"Did I ever tell you about how I wowed them in St. Louis with my rendition of *Hello Dolly*? I got three standing ovations. It was great."

To everyone's surprise, Cicie moved the tea trolley into the kitchen and then launched into *Hello Dolly*, using the full space of Bella's living room. When she had finished, the ladies jumped to their feet, applauding.

"Encore! Encore!" they cried.

"Alright," Cicie said, "but you have to join me. I mean it."

She got everyone on their feet and they marched around the living room, kicking their feet and swaying their arms as they sang *Hello Dolly*. When they had finished they flopped onto the couch and chairs, overcome with laughter, even Sandra. When Margarita got the hiccups, it sent them into another bout of giggles. At the moment when the laughter subsided and the room became still, Sandra spoke.

"I'm ready," she said. "Hold on to your hair, girls, because this is a hair-raiser."

Everyone shifted into an upright position to hear what she had to say. Bella jumped up and refreshed their drinks. When she was satisfied, she sat on the couch and said, "You have the floor, Sandra."

Sandra took a sip of her drink and sighed. Just

as she was about to open her mouth, the front door banged open and Josie came crashing through, her arms full of clothes, which she summarily dumped in the middle of the living room floor.

"They're Bennie's," she gasped, staggering to a chair and collapsing. "Bennie Uzul's. Someone get me a drink."

The women stared at her, open-mouthed.

Sandra was first to break the shocked silence. "Well, that trumps what I was going to say," she barked. "You've got the floor, Josie."

"And the pile on it," Boom Boom quipped.

"You knew him!" Margarita exploded, her face flushed. Two bright spots appeared on her prominent cheekbones. As a Filipina, her lineage and dedication to rigorous exercise kept her fit and toned, which belied her seventy-five years.

"Why do you have Bennie's clothes, Josie?" Mimi asked.

Josie gratefully accepted a Chardonnay from Bella. She took a gulp and choked on it. She started coughing and Cicie patted her on the back. When she caught her breath she said, "I need your help."

"Of course!" Veronica exclaimed.

"What's happened?" Cicie asked.

"Go on, honey. Tell us. We're all friends here," Bella said reassuringly.

"If I miss my guess, Josie just dumped a pile of

evidence on your floor, Bella," Sandra said, poking the toe of her sandal at a pair of jeans.

"I didn't know what else to do," Josie cried. "I went to the laundry room and checked, and there they were."

"How do you know where he left them?" Sweets asked.

Josie's face burned. "I was with him when he took them off."

"Holy crapola," Boom Boom swore, slapping her hand to her mouth.

"I don't understand," Cicie muttered. "Why would he do that?"

"Good grief, Cicie. You haven't forgotten sex, have you?" Sweets scoffed.

"You mean . . ."

"Yes, we were doing it on the washing machines. Bennie likes to wait for the spin cycle."

"Holy crapola!" Boom Boom howled, flabbergasted.

"How long?" Margarita asked, her lips trembling, her eyes boring a hole into Josie.

"Usually about ten minutes," Josie admitted.

"I mean how long have you and Bennie . . ."

"Oh. About six months."

"Six months!" Margarita gasped.

"Start at the beginning, Josie," Bella encouraged, looking pained.

"How d-did you m-meet him?" Mimi sputtered, covering her mouth.

Josie didn't notice the effect her words were having on her friends. She was gripped by a memory filled with pleasure and pain. Mimi looked as if she was having difficulty catching her breath and Margarita's eyes focused on Josie's forehead.

"He was working on my neighbor's down spout, putting in another one, I think. He had his shirt off. He had a very nice physique for an old guy. He was sweating, his chest was all glistening and sparkling in the sun."

"We get the picture, dear," Bella interrupted. "Go on."

"I was just being neighborly. I offered him a glass of iced tea. That's all. He came by an hour later to return the glass. David wasn't home. He didn't stay long, but he left me feeling things I haven't felt in years. I thought I was dead to all that. It has been years since David and I . . ." She stopped and took a gulp of wine.

She continued. "We met in the Laundromat every Wednesday. No one's ever around at four in the morning. Security doesn't come by until five, so we were never disturbed. David doesn't even know I'm gone. He sleeps 'til eight. We weren't there long. Like I said, just the spin cycle."

Cicie snorted her Manhattan through her nose. Sandra choked and started coughing. Mimi winced.

Veronica sucked vigorously on her margarita, trying hard not to look at Josie. Margarita's face was dark with disapproval. Boom Boom covered her face with her hands and made snorting noises. Sweets lost all control and laughed so hard she had to get up and go to the bathroom. Bella refilled Josie's glass.

"It's all right, Josie. Don't mind them," Veronica finally said. "He must have made you feel very special."

"Yes, that was it, exactly," Josie nodded, smiling up at her. "It was the thrill of it, you know. Not the act itself, but knowing someone desired me in that way again. He made me feel alive."

"Alive. Humph!" Margarita snuffed. Everyone ignored her.

"But what happened after that, Josie?" Sandra asked.

"Nothing. I left," she said. "The last time I saw him he was standing in his boxers, stretching his arms above his head in a tree pose. He had the most amazing physique. Did I say that already?" She sighed, and then started to cry. Cicie pushed a napkin into her hand. The room went quiet. All that could be heard was Josie whimpering and sniffing.

Sweets returned to the room and looked at the pieces of clothing on the floor. She looked at Josie, who appeared to be regaining her composure.

"Why did you bring his clothes here, Josie?" she asked.

"I panicked. When I heard what Maddie said that Gary said about him being in his boxer shorts, I just knew that I must have been the last person to see him alive. I thought all day about what I should do. I even took that detective's card. I was going to call him, and then I just had to know, so I went and looked. I found them in one of the dryers. I knew you were all meeting here, so I just grabbed them and came over. You have to help me! What am I going to do?"

"You need to tell Detective Varland," Sandra said. "He's not going to be happy because you've tampered with evidence, but he needs to know. Besides, Josie, you weren't the last person to see him alive. The killer was."

There was an audible gasp in the room. Margarita rushed out of the room.

"That's right! I wasn't! I didn't kill him!"

"Of course you didn't, and not only that," Veronica said, coming over and kneeling beside her, squeezing her arm, "but unless Bennie put his clothes in the dryer when you and he were, well, getting ready for the spin cycle, then someone else did."

"Why would someone do that?" Cicie asked. Her head was starting to spin. She looked at her empty glass. "Bella, could I have some water?"

"Good question, Cicie. I'll have another margarita,

if you have any left," Sandra stated. "Don't forget I've got something to say, as well."

"And bring in a plastic bag," Sweets shouted. "I think we should bag up these clothes. We're going to have to turn them over to the police. It's best we don't contaminate them any more than we have."

Bella returned with a bag in one hand and the pitcher of margarita mix in the other. She handed Sweets the bag and filled Sandra's glass.

"Where's Margarita?" Mimi asked, looking at all the women. There was the sound of the toilet flushing. Shortly, Margarita returned, looking ill.

"Are you okay, Margarita?" Bella inquired.

"Drank too fast," she mumbled and sat on the couch, folding her arms, avoiding eye contact.

"Okay, Sandra. It's your turn," Sweets said, once the clothes were bagged.

CHAPTER SIX

"I knew Bennie, too," Sandra began, quickly holding up her hand, "not in the way Josie did, but I had dealings with him. He was not my favorite person. Sorry, Josie. He threatened my John."

"Your husband?" Mimi asked, surprised. "What happened?"

"He wouldn't leave me alone," Sandra grimaced. She took a gulp of her drink, hiccupped and continued, "The first time I met him was at the St. Patrick's Day community dinner. Remember, we had corned beef and cabbage, steamed potatoes, and carrots?"

"And don't forget the k-key lime pie! D-didn't everyone l-love that p-pie?" Mimi stuttered.

"I was a server. I didn't know Bennie from Adam, but when he came through a second time, I noticed him. I watched him take his meal to the table and scrape it into a plastic container and put it in a bag. He hid it under his chair while he ate his first serving. When he came through a third time, I couldn't let it slide. I said, 'Hey, buddy, isn't this your third time through?' He said, 'what's it to you?' I said, 'I'm not going to serve you. You've already had two dinners for the price of one. You're not getting a third.' He cocked his finger at me and said, 'I'll remember you,' and then he took his bag and left."

"What a jerk," Cicie said, incensed. "I hate it when they take advantage of our community dinners. Don't they have their own food?"

"A lot of guys don't cook," Veronica grinned. "They store up food like squirrels."

"I was just mad at the time," Sandra continued. "A few months later, I was in the pool with my granddaughter. You remember when Lily came to visit. We were in the shallow end and you know how six-year-olds are; she got excited and did a cannonball. Bennie starts swearing at her. I was shocked. She's only six. Well, you know me, girls, I couldn't keep my mouth shut. I told him what I thought of him and it kind of escalated after that. He said, 'I remember you, Miss My Shit Don't Stink.' Sorry, girls, that's what he said. Then he said, 'Don't mess with me, or you'll be sorry!' It was very unpleasant. I would have said more, but Lily was there so I turned my back on him and took her home."

"I don't blame you," Veronica said hotly. "Did you report him?"

"Nah. I just decided to avoid him from then on, but he had other ideas."

"What do you mean?" Mimi asked.

"He started standing outside my house for no reason. Like when I'd go to our class, he'd be standing there on the other side of the street. Not doing anything, just making sure I knew he was there.

Sometimes he'd cock his finger at me, you know, like a gun. He'd leave after that. It was unnerving. I finally broke down and told John about it."

"What did he do?" Boom Boom asked.

"He was mad, but there was nothing he could do."

"I would hate that!" Sweets exclaimed. "I don't think I'd be that calm."

"What would you do?" Mimi asked her. "What could you do? There's nothing you can do with a stalker. They just won't go away."

"I'd . . . I'd . . . I don't know what I'd do!" Sweets gave up, exasperated.

"That's pretty much what we realized," Sandra continued. "Eventually he stopped doing it and we didn't see him that much. The last time we saw him was at the croquet field last week. John and I were playing with Maureen and Desmond Carpenter. You know, the new couple from South Dakota?"

"I know them. He's in the billiard league with David," Josie said.

"Well, Maureen whacked my ball off court. I went looking for it. He was there, standing behind a bush with his foot on my ball. I said, 'excuse me, that's my ball.' He said, 'figured you for two.' I was furious. I went back and got John. He was only too glad to confront the jerk.

"Their meeting wasn't good. It got a bit physical. John's not one to run from a fight and Bennie had been pushing our buttons for months. It was mostly shouting and shoving. John had the height and weight advantage and Bennie went down. I pulled John away. I didn't want him doing anything stupid.

"We were just leaving, when Bennie said, 'You'll be sorry. I'm going to get you.' John went back, put his foot on his face, pressed it into the dirt and said, 'you come near me or my wife and I'll kill you.' I don't know if anyone heard him, but that's what he said. And if that's not bad enough, Bennie stole his croquet mallet. We can't prove it, but we know he took it!

"Now, you see why I'm so upset? What if someone heard that? What if that detective interviews Maureen or Desmond? They were there. They could have heard what John said."

"Everyone knows John's a sweetheart," Boom Boom protested.

"You never know when a man is provoked," Sweets said.

"Sweets! You're not helping," Veronica scolded.

"All I'm saying is the guy deserved it," Sweets said. "If I were a man I'd have done the same thing."

"You don't mean that!" Cicie said, shocked. "He's a human being. No one has the right to take a life, no matter what the reason."

"Alright, alright. You're right, Cicie," Sweets said,

chagrined. "I was stalked once and it is maddening and frightening."

"You were?" Mimi asked, leaning forward. "Tell us."

"Yeah," Sweets continued. "The police can't help you unless he does something to you, and the stalker holds all the cards. He has all the power and you have none."

"What happened to him?" Mimi asked. "Your stalker?"

"Drafted and died in Viet Nam."

"That's one way to get rid of him, I guess," Mimi said. "So what now?"

"We call that nice detective as soon as possible," Boom Boom said.

"We can't! He'll arrest John!" Sandra shrieked.

"No, he won't. Where was John this morning between four and seven?" Boom Boom asked.

"In bed, with me. He left for tennis at six."

"Then he couldn't have killed him. Neither could you. Remember, Josie was with him from four to four-ten. Isn't that right, Josie? Ten minute spin cycle?"

"Not funny, Boom Boom" Josie slurred, gulping the rest of her wine. "Sometimes fifteen."

"And Alice found him when?"

"I don't know. Anyone?"

"Gary would know," Veronica said. "He fished him out. It would be before our class at seven. The cops were already there, so maybe six?"

"See Sandra, John has an alibi."

"What about Josie? What's her alibi?" Cicie asked.

All eyes turned to Josie. No one seemed to have an answer.

Just then, the doorbell rang. Bella went to the window and looked out.

"Can it! It's that detective," Bella hissed, shoving the bag of Bennie's clothes at Josie. "You and Sandra take these back to the Laundromat where you found them. Go out the back door. We'll distract him. Go!"

CHAPTER SEVEN

Detective Varland stood at Bella Adler's front door, waiting for her to answer. He hadn't had a chance to question her about what Alice Sheridan had said when she took her from the police car. He was hoping the old woman had been more lucid right after the crime than she had been when he'd seen her after her nap.

It was taking a while for someone to answer, but he could hear movement behind the door. He knocked again.

"Peralto Canyon Police," he said in his sternest tone.

Bella Adler opened the door. "Come in, Detective Varland. What brings you here?"

"Just need your statement, ma'am. You were with Mrs. Sheridan soon after she discovered the body."

"Why certainly, Detective. You remember these ladies?"

Varland was not expecting to run into the ladies from the aquatics club three times in one day. As soon as they saw him, they scurried around like hens scratching for seed. Each one of them suddenly had something they needed to do. It was pandemonium with all the goodbyes and hugs. Within a few minutes he was alone with his hostess.

"I'm sorry about that, Detective. We were just

having an afternoon libation. Would you care for a drink?"

"No thank you, ma'am. I won't take much of your time."

"Please sit down. Can I get you a glass of lemonade perhaps?"

"Alright."

He sat down in a comfortable wing chair and took out his notebook. Bella returned with a frosty glass of lemonade. He couldn't help but appreciate it. It had been a long, hot day with very little to show for it. The medical investigators had come back with zilch and the autopsy was taking longer than he'd expected. He drank deeply and set the glass down on the coffee table in front of the couch where Ms. Adler sat facing him.

"Thank you. That hit the spot. I appreciate your time. Mrs. Sheridan didn't have much to tell me," he began, "and I was hoping she said something to you."

"She was very upset. We all are. The only thing she said was that he was just like a starfish and he was dead."

"So he was in the pool when she found him."

"She just kept saying, 'dead, dead, dead.'"

"That's what she told me. You're sure that's all?"

Bella laughed. "Forgive me for laughing, but I

just remembered something she said. It's completely ridiculous, but she said it was a bat."

"A bat," he frowned, recalling the state of his witness.

"Yes, a bat. She said a big black bat killed him. I know, Detective Varland. She's not all there. You must have realized that when you talked to her."

"I did. Even if she had seen the killer, she wouldn't be the most reliable witness."

"I'm afraid so. Of course, she saw Gary, our maintenance man. She told him there was a body in the pool. He supposedly fished Bennie out with the pool hook."

Detective Varland jerked up his head and gave her an accusing stare. "How do you know that?"

Bella became flustered. "Ah, because he told one of the ladies."

"He did. Hmm," he responded. "Which lady?"

"Uhm, Madge, no Maddie. I'm sorry. I can't remember which."

"Can you get me both their names and unit numbers?"

"I guess so, but I'm sure they don't have anything to tell you."

"Let me be the judge of that. Did you know Benito Uzul, Mrs. Adler?"

"Call me Bella. I'm not married."

"Bella, did you know Mr. Uzul?"

There was the slightest hesitation as she said, "I didn't know Bennie Uzul."

"You're sure? Did you see him at the pool? Around the resort?"

Bella became flustered. She jumped up and retrieved the pitcher of lemonade and refilled his glass. "Would you care for some cheese and crackers?"

He smiled. There was something she wasn't telling him. "No thank you, Bella. Sit down and tell me what you know about Mr. Uzul. I have a feeling you're not being straight with me."

"How about I get you those numbers straight away before I forget."

"If you wish. And if it's not too much trouble, ma'am, could I have the rest of the names of the members of the Aquatics Club. If you have them?"

Bella was stunned. Why was he asking for that? "I don't understand," she said, feeling acid rise from the pit of her stomach.

"It might help in my investigation. Since you ladies were on the scene soon after the . . . incident, someone might have seen something that will help."

"I'm sure no one knows anything."

"All the same."

He waited for her to return with a piece of paper in her hand with fifteen names and unit numbers. He took it and she returned to the couch and clasped her hands in front of her. He waited for her to speak. The silence grew uncomfortable.

"Tell me how you know Bennie Uzul, Bella."

"You're very perceptive, Detective."

"That's what they pay me for."

"Yes, well, I knew him, but not from here. I only saw him a few times and thought I recognized him. When you said his name was Benito Uzul, I realized he must be the same guy I had worked with back in the day, only his name was Benito Ordaz then, not Uzul."

"Go on," he said, writing a note.

"It was years ago, when I was still working. I was an adman then, Detective. You know what that is?"

"Accountant?"

She laughed. "No, advertising exec. I was in Creative, designing ads and sets for commercials. There weren't many of us women working in that field back then. In fact, I was the only one who made exec."

"Congratulations. When was all this?"

"The fifties through the seventies, and thank you. I am rather proud of my accomplishments, but it wasn't given to me. I worked my ass off and it took thirty damn years. Oh, forgive me! I've had a little too much to drink and my language is the first to go." She giggled nervously.

"You were saying."

"I worked for Brittania Advertising. We had offices in San Francisco, New York and London. I worked in San Francisco. So did Benito. He wasn't there long. I believe he was fired for stealing. At least, that's what I heard."

"So you knew him."

"I knew of him. He was quite the masher. Always trying to pick up the secretaries and copy girls. They called him Don Juan behind his back because of his accent."

"But not you."

Bella blushed. "Okay, I admit it. He tried to pick me up once, but I wasn't his type. He was ten years my junior. Ballsy guy. I put him down pretty swiftly."

"How'd he take it?"

"Excuse me?"

"When you put him down, as you say, how'd he react? A guy with an ego like that must not have liked being put down."

Bella grew more uncomfortable. She began pulling on a thread at the hem of her blouse. She found a piece of lint on the couch, picked at it and twirled it between her fingers.

"Bella," Varland said gently, "tell me what happened."

She shook herself and stared defiantly at him. "If you must know, he assaulted me. But I was no pushover, Detective. I hit him in the head with a stapler and made my escape."

"Did you report him?"

"In those days, a woman kept her mouth shut, if she knew what was good for her and wanted to keep her job. A sexual assault was always attributed to the woman being too easy and 'asking for it.' It was a good old boy's network. They looked out for each other. I wasn't going to jeopardize my career, especially for a creep like him!"

"And when you saw him here at the resort and confronted him, did you still feel like clobbering him?"

"I . . . what do you mean? I did no such thing! I didn't speak to him here. I wasn't sure he was the same guy. Like I said, it was years ago. If that's everything, Detective Varland, I have to get ready for my glass working class."

She stood up. Detective Varland closed his notebook and stood up as well.

"Tell me something, Bella. How is it that you and Benito, I mean Bennie, ended up at the same place in Arizona after being in San Francisco all those years ago? Is it a coincidence or did you already know he was here and wanted to get your revenge?" He watched her carefully to see if he'd hit close to the truth.

Her eyes widened. "I'm sure you won't believe

me, Detective Varland, but it is just a coincidence. I did not plot to kill Benito."

"Really."

"Yes, really! It happens all the time here. I'll give you an example. A friend of mine from Idaho was walking to the clubhouse with her husband when they passed another couple coming their way. As they passed, they glanced at each other, but kept walking. My friend's husband said, 'I think that's my sister and brother-in-law from Michigan!' They turned around and saw the other couple staring at them. They hadn't seen each other for ten years and neither knew the other had moved to Superstition Way. I swear it's the truth. It happens all the time."

Varland wasn't sure he believed her, but it was a compelling story. "Fascinating. Well, thank you for your time, Bella. I appreciate you being candid with me. That's all for now. I'll be in touch."

"You'll . . . be in touch? I don't understand. Was there something more you needed?"

"You never know, " he said as he paused at the door. "It's early days. Early days."

He opened the door and went out. As the door shut, he stopped and looked at the paper. If he hurried, he might be able to catch the two ladies who Bella said had talked to the maintenance man. He heard a sound and listened. It sounded like she was crying on the other side of the door.

There was more there. He was sure of it. Poor old gal. It couldn't have been easy to be a career girl during the 50s and 60s. Even the 70s had its share of discrimination. That was when they had started introducing female detectives into the ranks. They had it rough.

Bella Adler was a tall, handsome woman even now in her golden years. He could imagine she was a looker fifty years earlier. She possibly had the strength to wield a weapon that would make a dent in Benito's skull—coincidence or not.

CHAPTER EIGHT

The air conditioning was working overtime, creating a low rumble, as Detective Varland entered the homicide squad room. The other two detectives were in their shirtsleeves, but he decided to keep his coat on. The contrast between 107 degrees outside and 78 degrees inside made him cold.

He was worn out and frustrated. He had just returned from the Forensics Lab in downtown Phoenix where he had witnessed the autopsy of Benito Uzul. The two surprises of the day were that there had been no water in the victim's lungs, indicating he was dead before he went into the pool, and the head wound, which had crushed the right side of his skull, had also been inflicted after death. He left Dr. Reginald Clement, the medical examiner, to further investigate the cause of death.

The Crime Scene Unit had been unable to find any forensic evidence at the scene. The place was immaculate. Exasperated, he had sent his officers out again to widen their search and canvas the people in the vicinity. The victim's clothes had to be somewhere since he didn't live in the park and he wasn't parading around in his underwear all the way from Costa del Grande to Superstition Way Resort. He also had them searching for a car. It had to be at the resort. Someone knew something. He just hadn't interviewed the right people.

The two old ladies had nothing to add. It was Maddie Ingersoll who had actually talked to the maintenance man, not Madge Ziegler, his first stop. Ms. Ziegler had kindly directed him to Mrs. Ingersoll's house and told him she was praying for the victim's family, if he had any. Her implied question hung in the air, but Varland let it hang. Their initial search for next-of-kin had so far turned up nothing. Apparently, the victim lived alone and hadn't listed anyone as an emergency contact at the Costa del Grande office. He had put Detective Mateo Garza on it.

Mrs. Ingersoll had been very sweet, but didn't have anything to add. She confirmed that she had spoken with "the pool guy". She couldn't remember his name, but he could find it easily enough. Before he left, she had insisted he take a sack saver that she had made herself. Supposedly he was to put plastic sacks into it.

He sat at his desk and pulled the blue cloth sack saver from his pocket. Neat idea. He'd always thrown his plastic sacks away. His thoughts wandered to the ladies of the Aquatics Club and he chuckled, shaking his head. He loosened his tie. The report from the medical investigators was on his desk in front of him, as well as the reports from the officers at the scene.

He put the sack saver in a drawer and reviewed them thoroughly. He picked up the phone.

"Clement. Varland. Got cause of death on Benito Uzul? Nothing yet? No, I'm not rushing you. Don't get into a snit, Clement! I just want to know what killed him. Some kind of poison? Okay, well, let me know as soon as you know. Yeah, yeah, poker's still on tomorrow. Guacamole? I don't know; oh, Jeanette's making it. Fine, then. Yes, I'll have chips. Later."

He hung up the phone and scratched his chin. He sat back in his chair and contemplated this new turn of events. His victim was dead when he went into the pool. How was that possible? Did someone carry him and lob him in? Did he fall in himself? Who conked him on his head after he was dead? Was it before or after he'd been poisoned? Poison! Was that why he'd fallen into the pool? Was there more than one person involved? There were lots of questions and for now, few answers.

He sighed. His simple case had just become complicated. Clement had speculated that the victim had died somewhere between midnight and six in the morning. According to Clement, it was difficult to tie down because the victim had been in the pool for at least an hour. What had happened before that was anybody's guess. He needed to talk to the maintenance man who had fished out the body. What was his name? He looked at the incident report and found the notation.

The phone rang and he picked it up. "Varland. Yes, Sergeant." He sat up in his chair. "Bring them to CSU immediately."

The victim's clothes had been found in a dryer at the resort's Laundromat. In addition, the medical investigators had found crumbs and cheese bits in the room off the laundry room and Benito Uzul's print on a plastic cup that was found under the couch. Now he was getting somewhere. Before he headed back to Superstition Way Resort, he stopped by Detective Garza's desk.

"Hey, Mateo, do me a favor, eh?"

"Sure, Magnus."

"Get me a background check on Benito Uzul, possibly known as Benito Ordaz. He might have some other aliases. Kind of a ladies man, you know. See if we have any paper on him. Oh, and here's a list of some of the residents. See if any of them have paper."

"Sure thing. Still on for tomorrow night?"

"Yeah. Clement is bringing his wife's guacamole. I've got chips."

"I'll bring the nuts."

"That's okay. I think Joey and Norm can find their own way."

Detective Garza snorted and went back to his computer to plug in the names Varland had given him. It was a long shot, but he had decided to follow a hunch. Those ladies from the Superstition Aquatics Club were too smug by half.

"I'm sorry I moved the body, sir," Gary Smith drawled.

They were seated in the main courtyard of the resort with cups of black coffee in front of them. The late afternoon sun was burning the back of their heads. There was no welcoming breeze. The air was so dry it sucked the moisture from their noses, making it difficult to breathe.

"Wasn't sure he was dead, was I? Soon as I pulled him out I seen he was. That's when I called Security."

"Did you know him?" Detective Varland asked, taking a sip of the coffee and inhaling the steam through his tender nostrils. It tasted surprisingly good and scorched his tongue. The sun was relentless on his back. He took off his suit coat and slung it over the arm of the chair next to him.

"Sure. I saw right off it was Bennie."

"How did you know him?"

"Oh, he works around the resort. I sometimes see him at the pool. Thinks he knows everything. Always giving advice, but he don't know squat. I've been working this place for twenty-five years. I don't need his no-good advice."

Gary Smith was a spry, wiry man in his early to mid-70s; it was hard to tell. He had light brown eyes that squinted in the sun, wispy brown hair cut short, and a narrow face with deep grooves from nose to mouth. He was dressed in khaki shirt and shorts and not a spot of perspiration appeared under his arms. Varland shifted his chair so his body would shadow the man's face. He could tell a lot from the way a man answered his questions. The problem was that it put his back directly into the sun. He could feel the skin under his shirt burning.

"You didn't care for him?"

"No, sir, I don't. He got on my nerves."

"Aggravating guy."

"You could say that again. Always butting in where he doesn't belong and hitting on the ladies, but when I come around, he'd stop and move on. We avoided each other. Only got into it the once."

"Tell me about that."

"Oh, it was nothing. Caught him in the Laundromat one morning and told him to get. He didn't take kindly."

"What was he doing there?"

"Washing his clothes, I guess. He was standing there in his boxers."

"When was this?"

"Couple weeks ago. This wasn't the first time,

Detective. A couple times I caught him stealing shower heads from the bath house."

"There were no theft charges against him."

"Didn't actually catch him at it, did I? Just that whenever he was around the pool, showerheads disappeared. I know it was him. Maddie told me that he put a new showerhead in her bathroom. Coincidence? I don't think so."

"You say you 'got into it' with him. What happened?"

"Nothing. I just told him to put on his clothes and get out. He told me to mind my own business. I told him it was my business. I look after the place. He said he wasn't going to leave. I said he was. He said . . ."

"I get it. Did you exchange blows?"

"Nothing like that. Just some pushing and shoving."

"Where were his clothes?"

"Now lemme think. I guess he put them on. That's right. He was putting them on while we was arguing."

"Where were they? You said he was doing laundry."

Gary stopped to think. "You know, now that you're asking, I'm thinking that they were sitting on top of one of the washers. I don't think he was washing his clothes after all. Maybe he's a pervert. Hell's bells! I never thought of that!"

"Anything else you can tell me about Bennie?" Varland was sweating profusely under his arms. He needed to wrap up this interview and get out of the sun. This sunburnt old guy didn't seem in any hurry to leave and appeared to have a resistance to heat. He was as cool as dry ice.

"Well, there was that one time . . . but that was long time ago."

"Tell me."

"Well, this is second-hand mind you, but I heard he was stalking a woman here in the resort."

"Do you know her name?"

"Mimi. Mimi Bradshaw. It's just a rumor, mind you, Detective, but I reckon it's probably true. She's a good looking woman."

"What'd you hear, Mr. Smith?"

"Well, as I heard it, he did some work for her and then wouldn't leave her alone. Hanging around her house, bugging her at the pool, stuff like that. Security started driving by her place to make sure she was alright."

"Did they catch him at it?"

"Nah. He's too cagey for that. It's pretty easy to slip between the units and hide. But I've heard he was kind of a nuisance to a lot of the ladies."

"Who'd you hear this rumor from, Mr. Smith?"

"Hmm. Lemme see. That's a difficult question to answer. The rumors around here are like a flood, picking up debris along the way. I guess I heard it from Ray; no, wait, Lexie; no, damn it, it was Sandra. That's it. She picks up all the gossip and usually gets her facts straight."

"Last name?"

"Fleming."

Detective Varland felt sweat trickle down his rib cage as he made a note of the name. It was time to go. He got up and picked up his coat.

"Thank you, Mr. Smith. I appreciate your time. If you think of anything else, let me know." He handed him his card.

"One thing I know is there's a lot of people here that won't be shedding tears for him. He was a damn nuisance and I'm not sorry he's gone. Whoops, I guess I better not say that. I saw the side of his head. I know it weren't no drowning."

"Let's keep that between us," Detective Varland said. "Oh, by the way, where were you between midnight and six this morning?"

"Lemme see. I guess I was sleeping until four and then went out to pick up trash. I do that every Wednesday."

"Can anyone corroborate that?"

"What? You mean alibi me? Saul Oberron. He goes out with me on pick-up day. Course, I sleep alone, more's the pity, so I guess I haven't an alibi from midnight to four. I didn't kill him, Detective, but I'll shake the hand of the man who did."

"You think it was a man?"

"Well, sure, don't you?"

"Thanks for the information, Mr. Smith. Oh, one more thing. Did Mr. Uzul have a foreign accent?"

"No. Talked regular. Didn't notice an accent."

Detective Varland left him in the courtyard and took another spin around the pool area. The water was very inviting. He could imagine himself in the pool, leisurely floating on foam noodles. He felt like jumping in with all his clothes on, but instead he veered over to the Laundromat.

The rooms were clean and tidy. There were two rows of washers back to back with dryers along one wall. There was a folding counter, which also served as a place to put flyers and pamphlets. He was surprised to find another room off the main room that looked more like a living room. It had a couch, a circular table with four chairs around it and a counter with two coffee urns, regular and decaf. Nice little private alcove for a midnight rendezvous. He poured himself a decaf and surveyed the room. The cup with Bennie's fingerprint must have come from under this couch. He bent down and looked under it. He would have to check with the office about access and use.

His cell phone rang.

"Detective Varland. Of course, I remember you,

Mrs. Ingersoll. I was just there. Yes, I love my sack saver. What can I do for you?"

Was this what it was going to be like? These old dears would fill up his time with useless conversations, calling him for no reason, plying him with cookies and cakes, making him little things. He had to admit it. He was putty in their hands. He was also going to get fat!

"Excuse me? Say that again? Yes, ma'am, I'll be right over."

CHAPTER NINE

Bella didn't want to admit to herself how much the detective's visit had rattled her. She hadn't cried like that in years. As she stood at the sink, she wiped her eyes with a cold washcloth and then put it against her forehead. She stared out the window.

In the distance was the purple mountain that looked like a rumpled pile of old laundry. The palm trees shook their shaggy green heads at the end of their long narrow necks. Across the street, Mr. Bradshaw was walking with his ailing wife who was using a wheeled walker. When Bella saw him lean over and kiss her on the cheek and her stopping to touch his face with her hand, she nearly started crying again.

"Get a hold of yourself, Bella," she admonished. "He can't hurt you now."

The tears started flowing again and a deep sob escaped her throat. It startled her like a slap in the face. She was in control of herself once again.

"What you need is to go shopping," she announced to the four walls.

She picked up her phone and dialed.

"Margarita, what are you doing? Have you eaten? How would you like to go to Bugsy's at the mall? We can get a bite to eat and then go shopping. You can? Great. I'll pick you up in half an hour."

Bella hung up. Her mood was exponentially lifted and she unconsciously began humming *I Left My Heart in San Francisco* as she got ready to go out.

"The spin cycle! I can't believe Josie would admit to it, let alone do it! What was she thinking?" Margarita said, waving an empty margarita glass in her hand. She was dressed in a red silk blouse that revealed her considerable cleavage. She was a stunning woman, even in her seventies. She had dark, curly hair and deep brown eyes that hinted at her Filipino heritage. She was normally a quiet woman, but when she drank she became voluble and dramatic.

"Maybe she was lonely," Bella shrugged as she took another bite of her shrimp. Bugsy's was one of their favorite places because they served three-dollar margaritas during happy hour and had a great selection of appetizers.

"Lonely! She's not lonely. She's got a husband. Not like you and me. I'm a widow and you're, well, you're single. We're not lonely."

"Sex, then. We all need sex."

"Bella! I'm shocked."

"I'm not dead yet, and neither are you! Don't tell me you don't miss it."

"I don't. I'm not interested. My husband was the only man I ever slept with. Since he died I haven't given it a moment's thought. Those days are gone. Sex! Who needs it?"

"I'm sorry. I didn't mean to make you feel bad."

"You didn't, Bella. I'm just upset that Josie was with that . . . that horrible man!"

"I didn't know you knew him, Margarita?"

Margarita choked on her chicken tender. She had a fit of coughing. She waved away Bella's offer of water as she wiped her mouth with a napkin. She cleared her throat. "What were we talking about?"

"Bennie Uzul."

"Oh, don't say that name! It leaves a foul taste on the tongue."

"Then, you did know him. Come on, Margarita. Don't hold out on me. We've never kept secrets from each other."

"I've got nothing to say."

"I'll tell you what. You tell me your secret and I'll tell you mine. Secret swear."

"I don't know what you mean. What secret do you have?"

Bella gave her that look; the one that always made Margarita spill her guts, especially when she had a couple drinks in her.

"I knew him," she admitted. She looked at her empty glass. "Where's that waitress?"

"How?"

"Please don't judge me, Bella!"

"I would never do that, sweetie." Bella reached over and patted Margarita's hand, beneath which she felt the large diamond wedding ring. "Go on. How do you know him?"

"I went out with him—but, only once! He took me to some nightclub in Phoenix. We went dancing. You know how Steven and I loved to dance. Ever since he's been gone, I've missed that most of all. When . . . that man . . . invited me—oh, I don't know what came over me, but I said yes."

"When was this?"

"About a month ago."

"Was it terrible, Margarita?"

"No, not too terrible. I hadn't laughed and danced like that in years. It was as if I were Cinderella at the ball—just for a moment to feel alive and young again, knowing that when the clock struck midnight I would go back to being lonely, old, pitiful Margarita again." She started to weep.

Bella sensed there was more and her stomach clutched with dread. She let her friend weep without interruption. It was short-lived as the waitress appeared and asked if they wanted anything more.

"Bring me another," Margarita mumbled, raising her empty glass.

After the waitress returned with her drink, a near unendurable silence of eating and drinking fell upon them. Margarita finally looked up at Bella, who was waiting with the patience of a saint, and said, "I miss Steven." A lone tear rolled down her cheek.

"I know you do, but you're not alone, Margarita. You have lots of friends. Many of them are widows. Reach out to them. Let them know you're hurting. They will embrace you like a sister. You know it's true. I'm your friend, Margarita."

"It's just not my way, you know. I'm a Filipina and we keep our feelings to ourselves. As long as I live I will never fully be an American. You know Steven was in the Army when he met me. I was only fifteen. Oh, he was so handsome, so open and funny. I fell in love instantly. My parents were furious and did everything to dissuade me. I think they knew even before I did that he would take me away from them."

"Have you ever been back?"

"Oh yes. But it is different now. You can't go home again. My parents are gone and I don't know my relatives anymore. It's a beautiful place, but no longer home."

"So now, where is home, Margarita?"

She stared at Bella as if she had a second head on her shoulder. Suddenly, her big brown eyes widened. Her perfectly formed lips spread to reveal white even teeth. When she smiled the cast of darkness fell off her like dissipating fog and once again she was a radiant woman with the exotic influence of her forebears. It was suddenly so obvious.

"I am home! This is my home! Why have I never seen it before, Bella? You've opened my eyes. I feel . . . I feel . . . like dancing!"

"Did you say dancing?" A deep voice spoke beside her.

They both looked up into the face of a very tan older man with dark eyebrows and gleaming black hair who was holding a business card out to her.

"Excuse me?"

"I'm sorry for interrupting you, but when I heard you say you felt like dancing, I wanted to give you my card. I have just opened a dance studio nearby and am looking for people to join. Interested?"

Margarita was dumbfounded. She stared at the man with her mouth slightly open, but she made no move to take his card. Bella reached over and took it from his fingers. "Thank you. We'll let you know."

The man nodded, smiled and moved on. Margarita didn't move.

"Hey! Are you okay?" Bella asked, worry filling her face once more. She waved her hand in front of Margarita's eyes.

Margarita blinked. "Did you see that man?"

"I'm right here."

"He looked . . . he looked . . . like a boy I knew."

"Back in the Philippines?"

"Yes."

"Here, take this. It's a sign."

Margarita took the card, looked at it, and started laughing. Bella joined her, relieved that her friend's dark mood had passed.

"I just might!" she said, putting the card in her purse. "And now, don't think I've forgotten. I've told you my secret, now you tell me yours."

Bella was disconcerted. Her desire to open up about her encounter with Benito Uzul was gone. With her friend looking so happy, she didn't want to bring back unhappy thoughts. She was sure as she was sitting there that Margarita's experience with him had been similar to her own. A leopard doesn't change his spots, even after fifty years! She improvised.

"It's about Moogie."

"What about her?"

"She's taken up with a married man."

"Again? Who is it this time?"

"You have to swear you won't say anything."

"I promise. Secret swear."

"Reggie Whitetower."

"Oh, that's old news. I heard it from Sweets."

"How about settling our bill. I want to go over to Carter and Lowe's and look at their swimwear."

The two ladies paid their bill and left the restaurant. As they entered the mall, Margarita grabbed Bella's arm, making her stop.

"He cheated on Josie with me, Bella. I'm not the least bit sad that he's dead," she whispered.

"Me, either, " Bella replied grimly.

"Are we terrible?"

"No. Just two gals shopping."

CHAPTER TEN

Driving into Superstition Way Resort, Detective Varland showed his badge to the surprised security guard at the gate, who quickly waved him through. He stopped and rolled down the passenger window. The guard stepped forward. She was a short, heavy-set woman, wearing a ball cap and a loose jacket with the resort's insignia and her name, "Gina" on a badge.

"Yes, sir? How can I help you?"

"Do you have a map and some information about the resort, Gina?"

"Certainly, sir."

She stepped into the guard shack and retrieved a map and a pamphlet, reaching in through the car window and handing them to him.

"Is there somewhere specifically you want to go, sir?" she asked, removing her ball cap, letting a cascade of brunette locks fall to her shoulders. She rested her arms on the passenger window and gave him a smile.

"I'm looking for Maddie Ingersoll's place."

"Maddie! You think she killed Bennie?"

He was startled that she had this information already, but then he remembered talking to the security guard, Bart Ferguson, that morning. Bad news travels fast.

He ignored her question. "How many people live here?"

"We have 1900 lots, about 1000 permanent units, the rest are open for RVs. During high season we have about 1800 people living here. This is low season, so there are only about 200 permanent residents here now."

"Did you know Bennie Uzul?"

"Sure. He came through here nearly every day."

"What kind of car did he drive?"

"Sorry. I don't know cars from cats. It was a big black SUV or something. If you need to know, I can call Bart. He knows everything."

"That'd be great."

While she contacted Bart, he reviewed the map and brochure.

"It's a Nissan Pathfinder," Gina said when she returned. "He thinks it's either a 2001 or 2002."

"Thanks for the information, Gina," he said, giving her a salute. She backed away and he drove on. He turned right at the first intersection and travelled nearly to the end of the street before turning left onto 12th Street.

Maddie Ingersoll paced the floor of her homey

living room, waiting for the detective to arrive. She had been beset with worry ever since he had come by to ask about what the pool guy had told her. He hadn't asked her if she knew Bennie, but after he left she felt like a criminal.

She was withholding information. That's what it was: withholding information in a criminal investigation. She knew that by watching her favorite show, *Matlock*. Could she go to jail for that? What would her children think if she were arrested? It would be disastrous! Her ten children each had spouses and children; five of them had grandchildren. It was the thought of their stricken faces when the police led her away in handcuffs that gave her the courage to call Detective Varland.

She occupied herself by setting out a plate of assorted cookies. Did he like tea or coffee? She decided to make both. Once she had the coffeemaker brewing, she put the kettle on the stove to make tea. What would he prefer? Green? English Breakfast? Darjeeling? When the kettle started sputtering, she filled a teapot with green tea. When that was accomplished, she sat in the living room and fidgeted.

What was she thinking? It was over 100 degrees outside! He would want something cold. She jumped up and opened the refrigerator. There was one bottle of beer that her son, Chris, had left. Did police officers drink on the job? Certainly not! No, he needed something non-alcoholic. She wracked her brain and came up with a packet of Lite Alive. She filled a pitcher with filtered water, added the sugary granules, and stirred. When it was dissolved, she added a tray of ice cubes. She stirred it again and then put it on the table. She found a tall glass and set it beside the pitcher. There. She was ready for him.

She was only five feet tall, and at 84, she was shrinking on an annual basis. Her thin white hair was cut short, but still wavy. Her face was surprisingly smooth and lightly wrinkled. Her carefully applied makeup enhanced her tiny, sparkling, sky blue eyes and little bow mouth. She had dressed herself in a stylish blue cotton dress, cinched at the waist. Blue beaded sandals completed her ensemble.

The doorbell chimed and she jumped.

Detective Varland entered when she opened the door. His stature filled the entryway. He was as tall as her oldest, Maxwell, but had the breadth of her third boy, William. His sandy colored hair was the same shade as Rachel's, her second oldest girl.

"Good evening, sir. Please come in. Thank you for coming right over."

"Quite alright, ma'am. You have some information for me?"

"Yes, I do. Please sit down. Would you care for some homemade cookies or something to drink? I have tea or coffee, or some iced flavored water or a beer. I don't know if you drink beer, but I have one in the fridge."

"I'm fine. Please sit down and tell me what you know about Benito Uzul."

Maddie tried not to show her disappointment. She came into the living room and sat down beside him on the couch.

"He was Bennie to me. I can't believe he's gone. So tragic! Can you tell me? Did he suffer?"

"I don't know. I'm not the pathologist. Tell me what you know about him. It will help our investigation."

"What did you say? I'm sorry, Detective. You'll have to speak up. I'm a bit deaf."

"I don't know," he said loudly.

"That's what I thought. I thought, I've got to tell Detective Varland because even though you didn't ask me if I knew him when you were over here before, I had to tell you that I did. I knew him very well."

"I'm glad you called me. Now, how do you know Benito?"

"Who?"

"Benito . . . Bennie. Bennie Uzul."

"Oh, yes, Bennie. At the pool about a year ago. He was so friendly. We got to talking. He reminded me of my fourth boy, Ricky. Tries so hard, but doesn't get anywhere. He was like a little dog lost. He had no luck at all. I felt sorry for him.

"First of all, his elderly mother was very ill and

needed surgery, but Medicare wouldn't pay for it. It's got to do with her back and she needed a mechanical spine or some such thing. I'm not sure what it's called, but it's very expensive. I appreciate a man who loves his mother, don't you?"

"Mmm. Certainly. Go on."

"A few months ago, his daughter's car broke down on her way out here to visit him, and she was stranded at a truck stop in Yuma. He was terrified something would happen to her. He would have gone to get her himself, but his car got wrecked by a drunk driver. He had to hitchhike into work and nobody knew this but me. I had to help him out."

"You say he had a daughter? What was her name?"

She stopped talking and frowned. Her face went blank.

"Mrs. Ingersoll?"

She shuddered and looked at him quizzically. "What did you ask me?"

"His daughter's name," he asked patiently.

"Whose daughter?"

"Bennie's."

"He had a daughter?"

"You said his daughter's car broke down in Yuma. Did he tell you her name?"

"I'm sorry. I can't remember. Maybe. Started with a B, no, a C. I don't know."

"Did you ever meet his mother, after helping her out with her operation?"

"Oh, no. She lives in Ohio. I just gave him the money. It was a success, though. She's much better. What were we talking about? Oh, yes! Bennie's luck. If you can believe it, his dog, Lucky, was poisoned by a neighbor because he said she was barking all the time. Only it wasn't Lucky, it was the dog next door! Lucky had to have emergency surgery. Can you imagine someone poisoning a dog?"

"Yes, I think I can. Go on."

"Well, Bennie says Lucky's his old self again. He was so grateful."

"Is that all of Bennie's misfortunes?"

"Oh no. During last year's monsoon a tree fell on his house and he had to get the roof fixed. I know. Can you believe his luck?"

"I think he got pretty lucky when he met you, Mrs. Ingersoll."

"Thank you. I did what I could for him, but his luck was changing. He was starting his own business. He got a pilot's license and was going to provide air taxi service; you know, for short local jumps."

"Don't tell me. All he needed was a plane."

"That's right! He looked for months, and all of a sudden the perfect one came on the market. He only needed $20,000. He said it was a steal because normally they go for $100,000."

"Did you give him the $20,000?"

"I was going to, but he . . . died. He won't need it any more, will he?"

"No, he won't. May I ask how much money you've given to Mr. Uzul?"

"Uhm, I don't know exactly, but I'd guess close to $15,000. I know that sounds like a lot, Detective Varland, but he needed it. He promised he would pay me back once his business was off the ground. We were going to be partners."

"Did anyone else know you were helping him financially?"

"You mean like my kids? No. I didn't tell them. I didn't tell anyone. Bennie was too embarrassed, so I told him I would keep it confidential."

"I'm sure he appreciated that. So, no one knew you were giving him money?"

"No. Well, Diddi did. She's my best friend. She told me not to trust him, but that's her. She doesn't trust anyone. And my son, Maxwell looks over my financial statements. He makes sure I have plenty of money in the bank so I don't overdraw."

"Did he ever ask you about these expenditures to Bennie?"

"Oh, no. He wouldn't. I always gave Bennie cash. That's the way he liked it because he said then he wouldn't have to declare it on his taxes."

"I'd like to talk to your son. Would you mind giving me his number?"

She got up and retrieved a piece of paper on the refrigerator with her son's cell phone number in large bold print. Varland wrote it down in his little notebook.

"I'm telling you, Detective Varland, Max doesn't know anything about Bennie. He wouldn't have liked me giving someone outside the family so much money. Neither would any of my kids. They have always had everything given to them and they don't understand what it's like to be poor and unlucky. My husband left me very well off and if I can help someone with it, I know Richard, that's my husband, would approve."

"Did he install a showerhead in your bathroom?"

"Why, how do you know that? Yes, he did, and he didn't even charge me. I tell you, Detective, he was a good, kind man."

"Where were you between midnight and six this morning, Mrs. Ingersoll."

She screwed up her face trying to process what he was asking her. "In bed. I get up at five to get ready for Aquatics Club."

"When was the last time you saw Benito?"

"Who?"

"Bennie"

"Oh, this last Sunday. I fed him dinner."

"Ah. What did you have?"

"His favorite. Chicken fried steak, mashed pota-toes and green beans. I also baked his favorite cookies. I always have them ready in case he drops by. Sometimes I give him a whole bagful. I still have some left. Would you like some?"

"I have to go, but I'll take some with me, if you'll wrap them up."

"Wonderful!" Maddie said, happily. She bustled into the kitchen and began wrapping up a dozen cookies.

"One more question, Mrs. Ingersoll. Do you have any poison in the house?"

"What a funny question, Detective. I don't think so. I did have a mouse problem, but Bennie took care of that for me. I don't like using poison because there are so many people here who have dogs. You know, they could eat it and die. I would never forgive myself if . . ."

"How did Bennie take care of your problem then?"

"I don't know, but I haven't seen any for awhile."

"Mind if I look?"

"No. I don't mind."

She watched as Varland looked under the sinks in the kitchen and bathroom, and stood at the door as he looked in her storage shed. He came back empty-handed. He practically ran into her when he re-entered the house. Up close, she decided that he was taller than Max and almost as good-looking. Almost.

"Thank you for your information, Mrs. Ingersoll. I'll be in touch."

"I feel so relieved. I wasn't sure if my information would be of any use to you, but I hope it will help you find out who killed him. He was such a dear, dear man."

"I'll let you know."

"Don't forget your cookies." She put the wrapped cookies into a blue star-spangled sack saver. She handed it to him, beaming with pleasure, and followed him to the front door.

"Detective, will you do me a favor?"

"If I can."

"Can you find out if Bennie's dog Lucky is okay? If no one wants him, I maybe could take him. I hate to think of him going to the pound. They kill them, you know."

"I can do that for you. Goodbye, Mrs. Ingersoll. Thanks for your help."

He went out the door and she watched him get into his car. As he drove away in the waning light, she breathed a sigh of relief. Now she could rest easy.

CHAPTER ELEVEN

The next morning Detective Varland drove to the Forensics Lab in downtown Phoenix. His nose twitched as it always did as he entered the special viewing room that had been created to allow law enforcement to view an autopsy without being exposed to biohazards. It was as if his nose could smell death through the glass.

He searched the empty room with his eyes until he found what he was looking for—a small, bony man in his late fifties, with thick white hair, hunched over a microscope in a corner of the room. He knocked on the window.

Dr. Reginald Clement, medical examiner for Maricopa County, looked up and peered at Varland without recognition. He pulled his glasses from the top of his head, adjusted them on his face and looked again. He smiled and gave a friendly wave. Varland entered the room, dangling a plastic bag full of cookies.

"For tonight?" Clement asked, smiling broadly.

"Evidence," Varland stated grimly.

"Too bad," the doctor responded, "they look tasty. Set them on the table over there."

"Check if they've been laced," Varland nodded,

setting the bag of Maddie Ingersoll's cookies on the table.

"Your murder suspect bakes cookies?"

"I sure hope not. She made me a sack saver."

"A what?"

"Never mind. Just being thorough. Anything new? You got his clothes?"

"I emailed a prelim to you. Didn't you read it?"

"Been out in the field."

"It's quite a good read. Very exciting. Looks as if your victim had sex before death. Semen stains on the inside of his t-shirt, but I can't be certain they're his until the DNA tests come back. Probably used his t-shirt for a towel. Go figure."

"Female partner?"

"Most likely. Depends on if he was a gentleman and let her use his shirt. I also found some biological residue on his pants. Waiting on the lab report."

"So no DNA yet."

"Good science takes time, Detective."

"I know. I was hoping for some evidence to direct my investigation."

"I've got one for you. I located a sliver of wood in the head wound."

"As in wood from a tree?"

"As in the weapon was made of wood, Detective; South American Massa to be exact."

"South American what?"

"Massa. It's a special red wood from South America used in construction, flooring, and—wait for it—croquet mallets."

"Are you saying he was hit with a croquet mallet?"

"That or a plank of Massa wood, but I'm not the detective. The wound pattern is more consistent with a mallet. I'd say if you find someone who owns a custom made croquet mallet of South American Massa, you will be closer to finding out who hit him on the head before he went into the pool."

"But he didn't drown."

"Dead when he went in."

"So you're pretty sure on the poison, then, not a fractured skull. Have you identified it?"

"It's in my report."

"Damn it, Clement! I've been busting my hump in near 110-degree heat while you sit here in your hermetically sealed, air conditioned room. I'm hot, sweaty, and I stink like a horse that's been rode hard and put away wet. I'm not in the mood."

"Whoa, cowboy, don't get your stirrups in a twist. Sheesh! I wondered what that odor was. To answer your question, it was strychnine. Usually used as rat poison. Ghastly way to die. Depending on the dose, death can result in ten minutes to two hours after ingestion. It causes seizures, severe hyperextension of the body and then asphyxia."

"TOD?"

"I've narrowed it between 4:00 and 6:00 yesterday morning. Difficult to be more accurate because of the temperature of the pool."

"So he ingested it, like he ate . . ."

"Cookies? I don't think so. Stomach contents did not include cookies. He was feasting on croissants, cheese and wine shortly before his death. The poison was most likely administered in the wine. Strychnine has a bitter taste, which can be disguised in red wine, Merlot, to be exact."

"Hmm. I think I know someone who likes Merlot. But, not cookies?"

"Not cookies. Shall I bring them tonight?"

"Well, if you're sure they're not evidence."

"I'm sure."

"Then that's a big ten-four."

After he left the forensics center, Detective Varland stopped in at Crazy Jim's for lunch. He took off his suit coat, and laid it on the seat opposite him. The air conditioning vent was right over his head and for once it was welcomed. It was already 100 degrees outside and not even 11 o'clock. He had been up since five and he was hungry. He ordered a Steak Picado Salad, loaded with thick steak slices, grilled onions, green peppers, cucumbers, pepperoncini's and jalapenos.

He washed down the fire with a large coke before he paid and headed for his next destination.

It didn't take long to locate Maxwell Ingersoll's office, since it was three blocks away in the government district downtown. Ingersoll was a busy deputy district attorney, but was more than anxious to talk about his mother.

He was a broad shouldered, square jawed, athlete in a business suit. He was good-looking, in his sixties and mildly pleasant. He ushered the detective into his inner sanctum and seated him in a large leather chair that reminded Varland of *Masterpiece Theater* for some reason. Maddie's son quickly sat behind his desk in a leather office chair and tented his fingers, schooling his features to reveal nothing.

"Now what's this you want to know about Mother's finances?"

Varland took his time before answering, staring out the window behind Ingersoll. It was a nice view of Phoenix from the 15th floor. It was a ploy he had learned over the years. Attorneys hated being on the defensive. They expected ready answers to their questions. When interviewing a lawyer, particularly a prominent deputy district attorney, he did his best to break the studied composure by allowing long pregnant pauses between questions.

"Do you know a man named Bennie Uzul, or Benito Uzul or possibly Benito Ordaz?"

"Never heard of him. Next?"

Varland slowly looked around the attorney's office. It was very masculine, but there were signs of his mother's decorations, hidden ever so inconspicuously in dark corners.

"Detective. I have a busy schedule today. What has my mother to do with this Uzul character?"

"She was giving him money. Lots of money."

"How do you know this?"

"She told me. Your mother's a very lovely person, Mr. Ingersoll, kind and generous, and perhaps a bit naive. Does she like to take in strays?"

Ingersoll sighed heavily. "More so since Dad died. Do you have a figure?"

"She estimates about $15,000 this year."

"That's impossible. I monitor her finances. I think I would know if she had made significant withdrawals."

"She's been giving him cash. I suspect he was scamming her."

"That's a kind word. If it's true, it's more like he was preying on an old lady. My mother's 84 years old, you know."

Varland let the comment hang in the air. He once again scanned the room as if he were looking for the murder weapon right then and there. He returned his eyes to Ingersoll and could see he was getting impatient. Time to lower the boom.

"So you're telling me you knew nothing about her plan to give him $20,000 to buy a plane?"

"What!" At that, the lawyer lost his composure and rose to his feet. His voice came out like a screech. "I'll murder the guy!"

"Is that a confession?" Varland asked quietly, giving the lawyer a beady stare.

The outrage went out of Ingersoll like a balloon losing air. He ran his hand through his luxurious salt-and-pepper hair and fell back into his chair. He glared at Varland, more for forcing him to lose control than for the disclosure he'd made.

"He's dead?"

"Murdered. Yesterday morning. At Superstition Way Resort. Your mother felt the need to confess to me that she knew the victim and had been rescuing him financially for almost a year."

Once again in control, the deputy district attorney spoke with authority. "Detective, you have me at a disadvantage. I know nothing of this. My mother withdraws increments of $500 rather regularly, sometimes a $1000, but she said it was for bingo."

"That's a lot of money to play bingo. Weren't you suspicious?"

The attorney managed a weak smile and spread his tented fingers in an act of surrender. "She has so few pleasures now. My father left her very well off, and I am rather indulgent on whatever makes her happy. But I had no idea she was being scammed. You can understand my feelings. The thought of some dirtbag taking advantage of my mother makes me furious."

"But not enough to kill him."

"Exactly, although if I'd known about it, I might have taken matters into my own hands. Don't misinterpret my words. I wouldn't have killed him, but I would have kicked him to the curb and cut off his access to my mother, legally. I'm sure you can understand that."

"I've met your mother, sir. She has a way of winning hearts."

Deputy District Attorney Ingersoll smiled boyishly. "She does that. We're a large family, Detective. You probably know that there are ten of us kids. We each have between us two to seven kids. Grandma is very much loved by her extended family. We do our best to protect her while giving her independence. The very thought of that guy . . . well, you can understand that it makes my skin crawl. I'll have to tell my siblings about it. We may need a family conference."

"I do understand. Where were you between four and six yesterday morning?"

"Getting ready for work. You can ask my wife. We rise early in our house. I've got fifteen-year-old twin daughters." He noticed Varland's raised eyebrows and laughed. "Late life surprises. We have two older boys and a girl, all married with kids of their own. But you're interested in my alibi, not my family. For most of that time I was stuck on the I-10. I conducted some business with my administrative assistant via cell phone. You can check with her and I'll make my phone records available, if you need them."

"Thank you for your time." Detective Varland was satisfied with what he'd learned and stood up. He stuck out his hand and shook Ingersoll's hand. He could see the mother's light blue eye color in the son's. He started for the door, with Ingersoll right behind him. He turned and confronted him once more.

"Do you have a sack saver?"

Ingersoll laughed. "One for every season."

Varland nodded, grinning, and left.

It was one o'clock by the time Varland returned to the squad room. It was nearly empty as Detectives Rinaldi and Luskowitz were out investigating or having lunch and Detective Brannon didn't clock in until five. He found Detective Garza eating a burrito at his desk. The guy was a geek through and through. He wasn't happy unless he was staring at a computer screen. He was a good detective, thorough, affable and a viper on cybercrime.

"Hey, Magnus," he said, through a mouthful. "Got the skinny on your vic."

"Oh, yeah?" Varland said, pulling up a chair.

"Yeah. You were right. Scam artist. First arrested in San Francisco in '73 for shoplifting. Appears to have beaten the charge and instead was given probation and ordered to attend a support group for kleptomaniacs. Who knew they had support groups for that. Anyway, after he completed his probation, seems to have jumped around a lot across the country. Things got hot, looks like he bailed. There were a couple outstanding warrants on him for theft. In 1974, he got a couple years in DC for selling pirated tapes of Pong. Remember Pong?"

"No. Go on."

"It was one of the first computer games. Like Ping-Pong."

"Mateo," Varland said, grinding his teeth.

"Sorry. Here's where it gets interesting. He was arrested, charged and convicted but he never served a day. For some reason his sentence was commuted and the warrants were expunged. After that, he just disappears. I'm working on tracking that down. Something fishy there."

"Good work, Mateo. Anything here in Arizona?"

"Not sure. All I've got is Benito Uzul applied for an Arizona license in 1995. I don't know when he changed his name. Appears he had all the paperwork: birth certificate, college transcripts, D.C. license. Probably bogus. I'm looking into that. Other than that, he seems to have been flying under the radar until last year. A restraining order was issued on him."

"Is that right? Who?"

"A Minuet Bradshaw. By the way, your Superstition ladies are clean."

"Figured."

"All except one."

Varland sat up in his chair. The news surprised him. "Who?"

"The same Minuet Bradshaw, aka Muirine O'Malley, aka Muirine O'Riley, aka Minuet O'Malley."

"What have you got on her?"

"Not much. Shoplifting charge in 1973 under the name Muirine O'Riley. No jail time. Court-ordered support group. Her lawyer successfully argued that she suffered from kleptomania. Something to do with deprivations after her lawyer husband Devlin O'Riley divorced her and pretty much left her penniless."

"What about that other alias? Muirine O'Malley."

"Name she was born with. Dublin, 1947. Her parents immigrated to the US in 1950. Married O'Riley in 1969. Divorced in 1971. Married Emmett Bradshaw in 1995. He died in 2012."

"And that last alias?"

"Ah, that was the name she took after she divorced O'Riley. It's a legal name change. She went from Muirine O'Riley to Minuet O'Malley."

"Sounds French."

"Nice though, eh? I'm thinking that if we have a girl; Minuet would be a nice name. What do you think?"

"Don't ask me. Ask your wife. Any paper on this Minuet O'Malley?"

"Nada. She worked as a high school teacher in Tempe until she married Bradshaw. Clean record."

"So other than the theft charges in 1973, she's clean."

"Yup."

"Thanks." Varland got up to leave.

"Don't you want to hear the best part? She and Benito Ordaz were in the same kleptomania support group in San Francisco in 1973. I know you didn't ask for it, but I did a little crosschecking to see if there was any connection. And, as I'm sure Minuet would say, 'Voila!'"

"You could have told me that first," Varland grumbled.

Detective Garza grinned and handed Varland a printout of his background searches.

Varland went to his office and reviewed the printout. Interesting. Mrs. Bradshaw's name had come up once before in his investigation. He looked at his notes and found it in his interview with Gary Smith. Mimi Bradshaw was the victim of Benito's stalking, according to Mr. Smith; probably the reason for the restraining order, which he noted with surprise was rescinded six months after being filed. However, the most interesting fact was that the two had known each other before. He recalled Bella Adler's story on coincidence, but as far as he was concerned prior history was motive in his book.

When Detective Joey Rinaldi returned from lunch, he sent him and Mateo to pick up Mrs. Bradshaw for questioning. If he were lucky, perhaps he could wrap up this murder investigation by dinnertime. He still had to run out and get the beer for the night's poker game.

CHAPTER TWELVE

Dawn broke over Superstition Way Resort, gradually brightening the trunks of the tall palms and casting their fronds forty feet above into stark relief against the sky's argent light. In the distance were the muted sounds of cars on the freeway as early morning commuters made their way into Phoenix. As dawn gave way, Great-tailed Grackles squawked from the trees, Mourning Doves cooed from their perches on the roofs, and a lone plane droned overhead. Other than that, it was as quiet as a theater before the curtain goes up.

"Hurry up! Get in here!" Sandra yelled out her front door as soon as Boom Boom and Madge drove up together in a golf cart. Cicie, with Babe sitting next to her, wasn't far behind in her cart, parking behind them. Josie, Sweets, Loretta and Margarita spilled out of Josie's mini-van. Bella came swerving around the corner, screeching to a halt, barely missing Veronica riding on her bike. Veronica righted her wheel just in time to scoot between Josie's mini-van and Cicie's golf cart.

"What's the emergency?" Veronica asked Josie as the two of them walked up the driveway to the front door where Sandra was beckoning urgently with her hand.

"I don't know. She just said it was bad and to meet at her house."

"Yeah, I got the same message." Veronica, her long hair in a ponytail, was wearing a multi-colored sundress. Josie was in contrast, wearing khaki shorts and a lacey khaki short-sleeved blouse. They both wore flip-flops.

"David had to wake me up. I never sleep in. We're usually in the pool by now."

"Where's Maddie and Diddi?" Sandra bellowed, as the two approached. They looked at each other and shrugged as one.

"Quit yelling, Sandra! Do you want the whole park to hear you?" Bella huffed, coming up behind them. She was dressed in black capris and a blousy black and white crossover top with sequins. "Maddie went to pick up Diddi. You know they don't move very fast. You're lucky you caught me. I was on my way to meet a friend for breakfast and a movie in Scottsdale."

"Which one?" Veronica asked, stepping back and holding the door for Bella and Josie. "Is it *Never Had Enough*? I heard it was good."

"No. *Cœur d'un Enfant*. French film. Means heart of a child."

"Oh, you're so highbrow, Bella," Sweets snickered as she settled next to Veronica on the floral couch in Sandra's living room. She was dressed in her usual denim jeans and shirt, her helmet on the floor beside her. "You won't catch me going to an art film. I like action adventure: *Terminator, Gladiator, The Expendables* . . ."

"*Easy Rider,*" Cicie laughed, nudging Josie, sitting next to her on the settee.

"I don't get it," Margarita said, rolling a kitchen chair into the room. Loretta was behind her, moving her chair over by the settee.

"We're not going to wait for Maddie and Diddi," Sandra said, standing in front of her friends. "This is too big. We have to decide what to do right away. It's outrageous! Simply outrageous!"

"Back the horse up a minute," Loretta admonished, putting her hands on Sandra's shoulders. "They don't know what's happened."

"You tell them then, Loretta. I'm too upset." Sandra left the room, but returned shortly with two folding chairs under her arms. She set them up and sat on one, crossing her arms. She wore cut-offs and a Hawaiian print shirt. Her blond bob framed her face, which was red with suppressed emotion.

Loretta stood next to Sandra and placed her hand on her friend's shoulder. Sandra sighed and unloosened her arms. Loretta was elegantly dressed in an ankle-length sun shift of shimmering blue material. Her short blond-streaked hair framed a narrow face with prominent cheekbones, pointed chin and serene blue eyes.

"Mimi's in trouble. She's in jail for Bennie Uzul's murder."

"What!"

"That's crazy!"

"Oh, my god!"

"She wouldn't!"

"What can we do?"

"Yes, what can we do?"

"We can pray," Madge admonished. She was standing against the wall, as she usually did. Her back was so bad that she felt better standing than sitting.

"I agree," Loretta said. "Madge, will you?"

"Let us bow our heads," Madge intoned, her voice dropping to a reverential level. The ladies obeyed without question. Every one of them had been the recipient of either Madge's or Loretta's prayers. Madge was a German refugee and Loretta a coal miner's daughter from the back woods of Virginia, but they were alike in their devotion to God.

"Heavenly Father, we don't understand what has happened to our friend, Mimi, but you do, Lord. Be with her and give her peace. Open the prison doors and set her free. In Jesus name, Amen."

"Amen," the ladies said in unison.

"Prayer's all well and good," Sandra fumed, "but we've got to figure out what to do and why the cops got it so wrong."

"But what can we do?" Cicie asked. "We're just a bunch of old ladies!"

"Speak for yourself," Sweets and Veronica said at the same time, and then started giggling.

"This is no laughing matter!" Sandra chided them. The ladies muffled their mirth.

"They must have had a reason," Babe asserted. "They don't arrest people without evidence. I know because my daughter's in the Secret Service."

Babe wore light purple slacks and a white print blouse, accented by an amethyst necklace and matching earrings. She was lying back in a recliner with her feet up. The neuropathy in her feet was getting worse, so she always propped them up whenever she could, and her friends always made sure she got the best chair.

"Bella knows. Mimi called her and we went to the jail last night. Go ahead and tell them," Loretta urged.

"This goes no further than this room," Bella commanded. She eyed her friends. They all nodded, some swallowing hard. "This is not common knowledge, but after she divorced her first husband, Mimi had a mental collapse which turned into some kind of kleptomania." There was an audible gasp in the room but Bella kept going. "She got caught shoplifting and the store pressed charges. Her lawyer got her off, but she had to agree to court-appointed counseling. That's where she met Bennie. It was a long time ago. In San

Francisco. She was only 26. You know as well as I do that she is nothing like that now. It's all in the past."

"I still don't understand," Babe retorted. "So what if she knew him once upon a time. That's no reason to arrest her for his murder."

"They also had a brief fling. Last year."

Josie gasped. Margarita's face paled. The rest of the ladies tried hard not to look shocked, but they were deeply affected.

"Still," Babe insisted, "that's no reason . . ."

"She got a restraining order against him," Loretta continued, sadly. "She said she was mortified when she ran into him here last year. She tried to avoid him, but he remembered her and wanted to start things up again. She turned him down flat. He started stalking her, harassing her. Security really couldn't do anything about it. Eventually, she got a restraining order. It was like fuel to the fire. He told her that if she didn't . . . I can't say it. Bella?"

Bella took up the tale. "He sort of forced himself on her through blackmail. He told her if she didn't sleep with him, he'd let everyone in the park know she was a thief and had been arrested. It frightened her and she, well, she complied. She went back to court and had the restraining order removed. She was now in bed with the enemy, so to speak."

"Poor Mimi!" Cicie cried. "I had no idea. She never said anything."

"She was too embarrassed. She didn't tell any of us. Not even me," Sandra sighed, dabbing her eyes with her fingertips. "I can't believe it."

"I'm afraid it gets worse," Bella continued. "Once he got his hooks into her, he took some compromising photos and started demanding money. Well, you know, Mimi; all she has is her husband's estate, but it isn't that large. She's only got Social Security with a small pension from her job as a teacher. He was bleeding her dry, threatening her very existence."

"And they found his fingerprint in her bedroom," Sandra whispered.

"Oh!" Josie cried, and covered her face in her hands.

"You're saying she has a motive," Babe ventured, speaking what everyone was thinking.

There was a brief silence, which was soon interrupted by the front door opening and Maddie and Diddi entering.

"What'd we miss?" Diddi asked, her voice wavering.

Maddie entered first, wearing pink capris, a pink Breast Cancer 10K t-shirt and a pink athletic cap. She helped Diddi over the doorstep and led her to a spot on the couch that Sweets had vacated.

Diddi was dressed in white gabardine slacks, a sky blue and white striped sailor top, and white deck shoes. Her hair was styled and her makeup was impeccable. She somewhat fell back into the couch against Veronica and adjusted herself until she was satisfied with her seat. At 95, she was still active, but age was catching up to her, although she fought hard to keep it at bay.

"What'd we miss?" Maddie asked as she took the last vacant folding chair.

"Mimi's been arrested."

"That's it? That's the big emergency?" Maddie snorted. "I think we all should be rested. I would have been too if Sandra hadn't made such a big fuss and got me out of bed."

"A-rrested, Maddie dear, as in, Mimi's in jail," Diddi shouted at her. "Why in the world is she in jail? What's happened?"

"She's in jail! What for?" Maddie exclaimed.

"Murder," Josie whispered.

"What's that? Speak up," Maddie shouted. "Her what?"

"Murder!" Sandra yelled. "She's been arrested for MURDER!"

"Don't shout, Sandra. I hear you fine," Maddie whined.

"Don't say it!" Boom Boom wailed, dabbing her eyes with a tissue. "You're making me crazy, Sandra! I don't want to hear you say that again about Mimi. There's no way. Just no way! She's the kindest, sweetest . . ." Words failed her and she blew her nose.

"She hasn't been arrested. They're just questioning her," Sweets said.

Maddie's pale face reddened with anger. "I'll call Maxwell right now and he'll straighten this all out. He's a deputy district attorney, you know. Where's a phone? Someone give me a phone. I'll call him right now."

"You can't," Sandra said, standing over Maddie so that she could hear. She looked chagrined and cast her eyes at Boom Boom's distress.

"Why not?" Maddie pouted. "He can help her."

"Yeah, why not, Sandra. It sounds like something we can do. At least he knows the law. We sure don't, I mean, I sure don't," Veronica nodded, looking at the other ladies for agreement. There appeared to be consensus all around.

"Because if we get the deputy district attorney involved, the media will be all over it," Sandra answered, "and then Mimi's secret will become common knowledge. It'll ruin her. She'll die from embarrassment. Imagine the gossip!"

"She has nothing to be ashamed of," Sweets said. "The guy was a predator. He stalked her and coerced her into having sex. If that had been me I'd . . ."

"Murder him?" Josie asked.

Sweets looked shocked but then nodded her head yes.

"Listen. If you remember what Bella told you,"

Sandra continued loudly so that Maddie could hear. "Mimi not only compromised her . . . virtue for that lowlife, but she paid him blackmail money. That's how much she wanted to keep this quiet!"

"Oh," Sweets said, nodding her head. "I forgot that."

"We all did," Loretta said in agreement. "We have to respect Mimi's wishes to keep this quiet, so I guess all we can do is keep her in our prayers."

"That's not all we can do!" Sandra argued, her blue eyes flashing, as she stood up once again. "Let's find the murderer and then they'll have to let her go!"

"I agree!" Cicie nodded. "I've said it all along . . ."

"He was a very bad man," Diddi broke in, her voice shaking with emotion, "and deserved to die."

"Diddi! No one deserves to die," Madge gasped, shocked.

"He did. He was a low-down, no-good, thieving, raping, traitorous swine," Diddi growled. Her voice seemed to fill the room and every woman fell silent, shocked by her vituperate words.

"Diddi, did you know him?" Sweets asked, barely forming the words.

"I'm too old for his kind. I'm just saying he was bad. Look what he did to Mimi."

"And don't forget that he was carrying on with Josie all the while and wasn't he stalking you and making your life miserable?" Veronica added, looking at Sandra.

Josie squirmed in her seat. Sandra looked pained and cleared her throat.

"You've got a point there, Diddi, and no one could have said it better'n you. Right here you've got Josie with a motive and me with a motive and don't forget my husband, John, how he threatened him."

"What are you saying, Sandra, that we should give ourselves up," Josie asked, her face drained of color.

"Of course not. You didn't kill him and neither did John or I. And Mimi didn't kill him. But somebody sure did, somebody here at the resort. Now we've got to put our heads together and think about who could have done it. Think, ladies. Think! We know almost everyone here. Somebody knows something."

"Alright, I have a confession to make," Madge blurted out, stepping away from the wall, looking grim. Everyone sat up and took notice. "I knew him, too."

"What! Madge, you, too?" Josie wailed. "You slept with him?"

"What?" Madge's eyes widened. "No! Of course not! He was going to church with me."

"Why, Madge! Why didn't you say something earlier?" Loretta chided.

"Because it was a spiritual matter," Madge stated emphatically. "He felt terrible guilt about the life he'd led. He was repentant. At least I thought he was. Honest, ladies, I didn't know anything about Mimi, or

Josie for that matter. He appeared to be a true seeker, at least that's what I thought."

"I don't believe it!" Maddie shouted. "He wasn't a peeper!"

"A seeker," Madge reiterated, "is one who seeks God, Maddie."

"Oh, right, seeker. Thought you said peeper, like a peeping Tom. He wasn't one of those. He wouldn't do anything like that."

"Right," Bella snorted. "Not our Bennie. He was a prince."

"Anyway," Madge continued, "he appeared genuine in his search for forgiveness. We prayed many nights together."

"Did he, by chance, take an offering?" Sweets asked, dreading Madge's answer.

"Excuse me? I don't know what you mean by that?"

"I mean did you give him money, Madge?"

Madge looked surprised. "Only now and again; just a few hundred dollars. He said he needed it and in Christian charity I gave it to him."

"I didn't catch that. What did Madge say?" Maddie asked.

"She said she gave Bennie a few hundred dollars!" Sweets said loudly. "Out of Christian charity."

"That's nothing. I gave him $12,000," Maddie said triumphantly.

"Oh no, Maddie, you didn't!" Cicie cried.

"Twelve thousand dollars!" Sweets exclaimed. "I could have paid off my Harley with that kind of dough! Why in the world did you do that, Maddie?"

"Because he needed it. And I would have given him $20,000 more if someone hadn't killed him, but not because of Christian charity, I'm afraid; it was business. He was going to start his own plane service and I was to be his partner!"

Again the ladies of the Superstition Aquatics Club were stunned by the confessions of their companions.

"Alright, that's it," Sandra said, pointing her finger at every one there. "Out with it. Anyone who had dealings with Bennie Uzul better speak now. And I want someone to keep notes. Veronica, will you do it? If we're going to catch this killer, we need to put our cards on the table. I want to know who else knew Bennie. You all know my story and Josie's. Now Madge's and Maddie's. Anyone else? Come on. Out with it. We're all friends here and it goes no further."

The ladies all looked around the room, barely daring to look each other in the eyes.

"Oh, alright, I'll come clean," Boom Boom announced, rolling in from the kitchen on the wheels of the kitchen chair. "I was hoping I could keep this to myself, but if it's confession time, being a good Catholic, I can't help myself. So, I hired the bum to set up my TV/sound system. We used to watch baseball together. I gave him eight grand. There! I've said it!

End of story! Oh, and I didn't kill him!" She crossed her arms and legs and no one could get anything more from her, even though the ladies cajoled and begged her for details.

Sandra once again took control. "So it appears Bennie was scamming and bothering a lot of us. There must be even more than us here. There's motive."

"Well, I didn't give him any money," Cicie piped up, "but I did give him free piano lessons. After I learned he was dead, I got to thinking he wasn't such a good guy. I took a look and sure enough some of my jewelry and my husband's gold watch are gone. You think it was Bennie?"

"Of course it was him!" Diddi shouted.

"Anyone else?" Sandra asked. "Babe?"

"Never met him."

"Sweets?"

"Nope."

"Veronica?"

"I wish I had. I'd have taken him out with one chop to the kneecaps!"

"Bella?"

"No."

"Margarita?"

An exchange of looks took place between Bella and Margarita. All she could do was shake her head no.

"That's it then," Sandra concluded. "It's not one of us, so it has to be someone else. My guess is it was

someone from the resort. I want each of us to investigate on our own. Find out what you can. Loretta, you
used to work in the office. See if Regina has any intel."

"Who tells?"

"Intel, Maddie. Intelligence. Information. Facts."

"You don't need to shout. I can hear you."

"I'll pump Gary for information. I heard he was
talking to that detective," Sweets said.

"I have a friend in the police department,"
Veronica said, conspiratorially. "Maybe I can find out
something from her."

"Good idea," Sandra agreed.

"And I'll talk to Reverend Julian," Madge volunteered. "He may be willing to tell me about Bennie.
He'll be so upset. He was already arranging his bap-
tism. Bennie promised to give the church $50,000.
We were going to use it to buy a bus for the school. I
just can't believe I was so wrong about him. Serpents
disguised as doves. Oh, it makes me so mad!"

"I'll talk to Rosalie," Josie offered. "We're in the
same bridge club."

"That's a great idea," Sandra agreed. "If it's
happening at the resort, Rosalie Hunter will know
about it."

"I can talk to my daughter," Babe suggested. "She
won't know anything about the guy, but she might
give us some advice on how to go about locating his
killer. Did I tell you she's a federal agent?"

"Several times, Babe. I'll invite that nice detective over for a glass of Merlot," Boom Boom offered. "If I can't find out what he knows, I'll be Boom Boom no longer."

"Be careful, Boom Boom," Veronica warned. "He's a detective. This isn't a game."

"You let me worry about that. I've had plenty of dealings with the cops. Of course it's not a game, Veronica, but I still know how to play."

"I'm not even going to ask," Sweets snickered. "You always surprise me, Boom Boom."

"Anyone else?" Sandra redirected the group's attention.

"I can talk to my son. He's the deputy district attorney."

"We already said no to that, Maddie. Why don't you talk to Laura in the Activities Office? She might have run across him. He did a lot of work here. She might have some information."

"Okay. I like Laura. I'll do that. Diddi, do you want to come with me?"

Diddi nodded. She was looking grim-faced. Her arms were crossed and her shoulders were hunched as if she were trying to stay warm.

"Okay, then, I think we've got our assignments. Remember. Not a word about Mimi. Make discreet inquiries. Operative word: discreet. We don't want to tip anyone off that we're looking into this murder.

And write it down as soon as you can. I don't want any of us to rely on our memories."

"What are you saying, Sandra? That we're getting old?"

"I'm saying that we have difficulty remembering things."

"It's a very good idea, Sandra," Veronica agreed. "I'll be happy to check on Mimi. She could probably use a friendly face."

"I have some cookies you can take to her," Maddie offered.

"Maybe she would like a sweater. It's probably cold in jail," Cicie said, speaking to Veronica. "I have the key to her house."

"Alright, alright! We know what we have to do. Let's meet tomorrow at our regular swim time, only in the courtyard. We can have our coffee and compare notes. Babe, will you do the honors?"

Babe pushed the control on the chair and it swung upright. "This meeting of the Superstition Murder Club is adjourned!"

CHAPTER THIRTEEN

It had been a busy morning for Detective Varland and he was hot, sweaty and frustrated.

He had gone to Costa del Grande where Bennie Uzul lived to talk directly to the resort's manager, Cyrus Lippenschift. Not surprisingly, the man knew nothing about Benito Uzul. All he learned was that Bennie had resided at the resort for ten years. He got a copy of his residency application. There was no emergency contact listed, no credible employment; he was "self-employed." There was a bank account listed and he called Detective Garza to check it out.

He had talked to Bennie's neighbors on either side of his house; Georgia and Phil Crasta in #142 and Raul and Pilar Gomez in #146, but they knew almost nothing about him. They were both very nice couples and, as most retired people, kept tabs on their neighbors. They knew all about the man across the street in Unit #145 who was a retired engineer who had recently lost his wife to cancer, and the woman in Unit #147 was bed-ridden and had a home health aide worker come in once a day; but the man who lived at #144, Bennie Uzul, was a mystery to them. All they could say for sure was that he was gone most days and came home usually after they'd gone to bed. He kept to himself and was friendly enough when they saw him, but he didn't stay to talk. He didn't go to their parties and they never saw him at the resort events. They knew he was home only by the smell of cigarette smoke in the air. They did know that he drove a black 2002 Nissan Pathfinder. It was loud and obnoxious, they said.

After that, he had interviewed Linda Hoffman, general manager of Superstition Way Resort. She was a smart, efficient woman in her early forties. She had beautiful long hair, a pretty, friendly face and an engaging personality. She was also extremely busy. While he waited for her to finish with a resident who demanded that she explain his recent bill, he observed that the office was in a constant state of motion. People entered and departed in a steady stream. The office staff was quick to respond to inquiries, sign-ins, sign-outs, complaints, requests for maps, brochures and by-laws, and incredibly patient when a resident appeared to have no other business than to waste their time.

When he did get to sit down with Ms. Hoffman, she had little to tell him. She was not very happy that he had closed off the pool. She had been fielding phone calls and complaints all day. She accepted his explanation, but he could tell her patience would not last long. The pools were essential to the happiness of the residents.

All he learned from her was that Bennie had been an approved vendor who offered handyman services to the residents. However, since he had two complaints against him noted in the security log, his access to the park was recently revoked. The residents in #1750 and #1751 had repeatedly asked him not to park his car in front of their houses. It was against resort policy to park on the streets and his vehicle was noisy. They had finally made an official complaint.

Varland noted that Unit #1751 was the residence of David and Josie Simone. He checked his list and confirmed that Josie Simone was one of the ladies in the Aquatics Club that had violated his crime scene. He couldn't quite place her face.

The other complaint was from a woman at Unit #590 for his use of foul language. It appeared that Patton, a Schnauzer, didn't care for Bennie and would bark every time he walked by. Bennie didn't care for Patton either and one day let out a torrent of swear words that Mrs. Greenfeld said was enough to "make her aluminum siding curl."

There was also a request from Mimi Bradshaw that Security patrol her street because Bennie Uzul was "bothering her." Ms. Hoffman stated that due to these complaints, his entry privileges had been revoked the week before. Security had been alerted to keep him out of the resort. Obviously, that had not been successful, and Linda was embarrassed and apologetic.

As far as access to the Laundromat, she told him that it was always unlocked. Security patrolled it every two hours, but they didn't check to see if the people using it were from the resort. It was pretty much open for use 24/7.

With this information, he had thanked Ms. Hoffman for her time and reluctantly accepted from her the list of homes available for rent or sale at the resort, with a promise that he would think about it. When he had left the air-conditioned office and entered the blistering heat outdoors, he had thought of the resort's many amenities, especially the azure pool and its siren song.

No one had been home at the Simone house. He had left his card with a note on it to give him a call. He didn't expect much from it, but perhaps the couple had met Bennie and had further information. He had assigned Detective Luskowitz to follow up on them and on Sandra Fleming, who had been the source of Gary Smith's statement that Bennie had stalked Mrs. Bradshaw.

Sitting in his office, sipping on a cup of horrid coffee (nothing like the delicious free coffee at the resort), he contemplated the case. It was now three days since the murder and he had one suspect in custody on suspicion of murder.

Mimi Bradshaw's lawyer was due in at any moment and he knew he would lose her then. She hadn't confessed and there was scant evidence to hold her. It was true that she had no alibi from 4:00 to 6:00 a.m. "I was sleeping alone," she had said, but she had been at the pool at seven, along with the other ladies from the Aquatics Club who would all confirm her attendance. He had no doubt of that. She didn't seem cold-blooded enough to have killed him and then gone to her exercise class. But, in his experience, you never ruled anyone out because people were sometimes driven to do unexpected and horrific things. She was still his best suspect. Unfortunately, she was his only suspect.

Thankfully, she was cooperative and had allowed him to do a search of her house.

"I have nothing to hide—now," she had said forlornly. "My reputation is ruined, thanks to you."

As pleased as he had been to have immediate access to her house, it had yielded little. His team had found no rat poison, no croquet mallet and no plank of Matta wood. All he had was one lousy fingerprint, a restraining order, a weak blackmail motive and a dead body. As soon as her lawyer arrived, she would be released.

The forensic investigators had lifted only one of Bennie's prints from her house. It was found on the footboard of her bed. It was evidence but only confirmed Bennie had been there, not that she'd killed him. The lack of Bennie's fingerprints bothered him.

It was highly unlikely that with him being in her house several times, as she herself admitted, he would leave only one solitary print. Bradshaw's prints were all over the house, along with several unidentified prints. Since she entertained frequently, there was no point to printing the entire resort to identify them. They were being processed anyway—just in case someone had a record. He was pretty sure Bennie had not been killed at her house, so it was a moot point. For now, it was enough that he had another one of Bennie's prints, which matched the one on the plastic cup found in the Laundromat.

When questioned, Bradshaw couldn't remember the last time she'd polished her bedroom furniture. As far as she knew, it had been six months since Bennie had been in her house. He had asked her if she had wiped everything down after Bennie's visits?

"As much as that idea appeals to me, Detective, the only thing I will confess to is that I'm a lousy housekeeper. My idea of cleaning is to vacuum the rugs and wipe down the kitchen counters. I only scrub the floors when my shoes start sticking. As for wiping down my furniture, I'd have to say rarely— maybe after a dust storm, but really, what's the point? There's always more dust."

Why only the one print left in her house? It was suspicious. If Bennie had been in her house as much as she said, where were his prints? If Mimi wasn't wiping things down, then could it be that Bennie had wiped down his own prints? Why would he do that? It was odd, to say the least. Who was this guy, anyway?

That wasn't his only problem. The forensic investigators had thoroughly searched Bennie's house and came up empty, and it was that emptiness that had Varland even more stumped. Bennie's house was antiseptically clean and tidy. It almost looked as if he didn't live there. The investigators had never seen a place so devoid of fingerprints or hair. They didn't find a hairbrush, a comb or a razor. There wasn't a calendar, correspondence of any kind or personal notes. The only pictures on the wall in the small, single-wide mobile home were framed landscapes. There were no personal photos on display. The bedroom closet had a few items of clothing and a couple pair of shoes, which they'd bagged. They did find a hall closet full of bleach and cleaning supplies. The vacuum cleaner had been washed clean.

Again he wondered what was behind Bennie's suspicious actions? As far as Varland was concerned, he was either a clean freak or hiding something from a dark past. He suspected the latter. Why else would he go to such lengths to eradiate his prints and DNA? He messed up, though. Twice. He had left a print on a plastic glass and one at Mimi's.

Without any other suspects, he was hoping he could hold Mimi Bradshaw long enough for the DNA analysis. If he could tie her to the victim within the TOD, he would formally charge her with murder. His phone rang.

"Varland. What do you have for me, Clement? So, the plastic glass contained Merlot? And strychnine. Got it. Yes, that helps. All right, I'll come by later. Oh, and please tell Jeanette her guacamole was a success. We all appreciate eating her culinary experiments. What kind of sandwiches? Do they go with beer? Okay, bring them next week. See you."

Just as he hung up, there was a knock on his door and Detective Joey Rinaldi peered in. Varland beckoned him to enter. He was a good-looking, slightly built man in his thirties with shiny, thick black hair, combed back. One strand invariably fell forward and he had a habit of smoothing it back. Today he wore a light gray suit jacket over a light blue polo shirt.

"Got something for you," he grinned, standing at ease in front of him. "We found the car. Thought you might like to see it for yourself."

Detective Varland followed him into the garage off the impound yard where a 2002 Nissan Pathfinder was being searched. The investigators stepped back as Varland followed Rinaldi to the back of the vehicle. The hatch was open and inside was all of Bennie Uzul's personal possessions. He nodded to the investigators and watched as the team removed and filed into evidence two suitcases, a duffel bag, a plastic storage container filled with files, a metal security box and a one-man tent. Once these were removed and taken to the Crime Scene Unit, they opened the Pathfinder's back doors and removed and filed into evidence a sleeping bag, pillow, foam mat, camp stove, two flashlights, pack of D batteries, camp light, cooler, hydration back pack, and two sacks full of groceries. On the passenger seat were two maps, one for Arizona, and one for Utah.

Varland pulled latex gloves from his pocket, put them on and picked up the Arizona map. He opened it and spread it out.

"Rinaldi. Come here. Where is that?" he indicated a spot on the map with his head.

Rinaldi leaned across his arms and peered at the map.

"Looks like he's circled Stateline Campground. I know that area. It's very remote. Part of the Vermillion Cliffs on the Grand Staircase. Near the Grand Canyon. Very primitive area. For serious hikers. There are trails that lead from Arizona into Utah."

Varland folded the map and handed if off to the investigators. "On the border, eh?"

"Yup. I'm going to take a stab and say it looks like old Bennie was about to do a runner," Rinaldi grinned, his even white teeth gleaming in the artificial light. "Didn't you say he was about to come into 20 grand? Maybe he was through fleecing the old lady and was looking to lay low for awhile."

"Possibly." Varland clapped his hand on Rinaldi's shoulder. "Good work. Where'd you find the car?"

"Safeway parking lot; about a half mile from the resort. There's an access trail from the resort to the back of the store. Residents go over in their golf carts. Looks like old Bennie used it to sneak in. Don't know why he didn't drive through the gate like usual, but looks like he was ready to hightail it."

"Only someone stopped him."

"Yup, and I'm guessing it's not the Ingersoll woman."

"Mrs. Ingersoll didn't kill him, and I'm not sure Mrs. Bradshaw did either. There's something we're missing. Something hidden."

"What's that, Magnus? Your gut acting up again?"

He smiled. His gut instincts were a constant source of amusement within the squad. "Time will tell. By the looks of this, I'd say he wasn't just planning to leave, he was planning to disappear."

"Disappear?" Rinaldi inquired.

"Given where he was going; remote, primitive, you say, and an easy border crossing."

"You're right."

"I don't like it. I don't like it at all."

"Why?"

"Because we've got more work to do. There's another motive here that I can't see. He was a creep and a grifter, but also a pro at hiding his whereabouts for some reason, and I don't think it was the law he was afraid of. Something else."

"I'm not following."

"He was heading for the hills, literally, because something or someone had spooked him. Someone who likes to drink Merlot, perhaps."

Chapter Fourteen

Boom Boom was finishing the last touches on her oil painting when her doorbell rang. She scowled at the interruption. The flower arrangement was starting to wilt and she was having difficulty remembering its vibrant colors, which were now all faded and muted. Some of the petals were already on the floor. She wiped her brush with a turpentine cloth and set it down. She tiptoed to the door and looked through the peephole. She immediately flung it open.

"Why, Chief Varland! What a pleasant surprise. Please come in. I must look a fright! I wasn't expecting company. Please, please come in."

The detective entered the room and she instantly saw her living room through his eyes. It was a holy mess. Newspapers were placed all over the floor and furniture because she had a tendency to flick her paintbrush and drop great globs of paint on the floor when she squeezed the tubes onto her pallet. Her easel took up most of the room and the flowers on the canvas appeared to be listing to one side. She quickly threw a covering over her painting, while at the same time realized she was wearing a paint-spattered smock. She shrugged it off and laid it over the back of a chair. She was dressed in an off-the-shoulder black tank and black leggings.

"Excuse the mess," she apologized, patting her hair into place. She could tell by the feel of it that it was sticking up on one side. "I'm rushing to finish this for our annual art show."

"Excuse me?" the detective shouted.

She realized her television was blaring with her favorite soap opera. She scurried around the room, avoiding the paint-spattered newspapers, searching for the remote. The detective found it on the kitchen table and muted the sound.

"That's better," he said and smiled indulgently. "I was wondering if we could talk."

"Why of course! I'm honored that you should think I have something to say. It's about the murder, of course. Please, sit down."

She indicated a kitchen chair and before he could sit, she quickly moved in to remove her cat, a gray, shorthaired tabby that was none too happy about having his nap interrupted. He yowled and scampered down the hallway.

"That's Kissy-poo," she giggled. "He doesn't like men, I'm afraid."

"Ms. Klutterbuck, please sit down. I won't take much of your time."

"Oh, you must call me Boom Boom. Everyone I like does and I like you, Chief."

She sat opposite him and gave him a seductive smile. She leaned into him.

The batting of her eyes disconcerted him. "Boom Boom is a very unusual name."

"That's my stage name. If you promise not to tell anyone, my real name is Gertrude. Ugh! What an awful name. Gertrude Klutterbuck. You can see why I had to change it."

"You were on the stage?"

"Well, that's what I tell people here, but, to be honest, I was more of an exotic dancer. A pole dancer, to be exact. I know I don't look like it now, but in my day I was quite athletic and a real beauty. I worked all the best clubs in Vegas and Phoenix. I was at the Light Fantastic Lounge in Vegas until I had to have my hip replaced. Once I got back in shape, I got another gig at Monty's, but then I had to have a second hip replacement and it was curtains for me. I've been retired for about twenty-five years. Goodness! That sounds like a long time ago, doesn't it?"

"Yes, well, uhm, the reason I want to talk to you is to find out what you can tell me about Benito Uzul. I have a feeling you knew him."

"Bennie. Humph! What a piece of work he is, I mean, was. I know I shouldn't speak ill of the dead, but he was a royal piece of sh-slime, Chief Varland. I'm not sorry he's dead. There! I've said it!"

"You didn't like him."

"Who did? Well, that's not really true. Lots of the ladies liked him. At first he comes across as a big, helpful guy, and he was easy on the eyes, even at seventy. He had a way of making you feel, oh, I don't know, important. I admit I was taken in by him."

"How so?"

"One of my, uh, 'admirers' bought me that television and DVD player for my birthday; I turned eighty-seven in February. I know, I know, you can't believe it. I'm like a fine wine, you know. I age well. Don't you think?"

"You were saying . . ."

"What was I saying?"

"About how you got involved with Bennie."

"Involved. Was I? Yes, I guess I was, but not like Josie. It all had to do with that television. Isn't it lovely? I get all the games. Do you play sports, Chief? You look like you do. You really are a very handsome man. Did you know that? Are you married?"

"Who's Josie?"

"What?"

"You said, 'not like Josie.' Who's Josie?"

"Did I? I meant to say cozy, as in I wasn't cozy with him. Do I have to spell it out for you, Chief?"

That seemed to satisfy him. "Please go on, Boom Boom."

"I'm sorry. I'm just not used to having such a dashing gentleman call on me, and here I am, such a frightful mess! I'm all twitterpated!"

"Ms. Klutterbuck, please!"

"What? Oh! Now, what was I saying? Oh yes, the television. Well, I didn't know anything about how to get them to work. One of my, uh, friends recommended Bennie. He came over and set it all up. From then on we watched the Diamondbacks every time they televised the game. Are you a baseball fan, Chief?"

"So, you watched the games with Mr. Uzul."

"Yes, every time they televised it. He would come over and we'd watch the game. I always had a bottle of wine for him. He liked Merlot. Me, too. It's my favorite. Do you drink wine, Chief?"

"Beer drinker, I'm afraid."

"Oh dear, well that can't be helped."

"So you always supplied the wine."

"Of course. I try to be a good hostess. Would you care for a glass? Oops, no, you like beer. I'm afraid I haven't got any. Would you like a glass of water, or something stronger? I think I've got some Scotch."

"I'm fine, thank you. Tell me, did you buy your wine for every game, or do you keep it on hand."

She looked puzzled at first but then brightened. "There are so many games, you know, Chief, that I buy it by the case. I just bought some, but now that Bennie's no longer with us, I guess I'll have to find someone else to drink with. Too bad you don't drink wine, Chief. Maybe I can convert you?"

"Many have tried and failed," he smiled at her.

His eyes were glittering and she wondered if he would make a move on her. She could only dream.

"That's why I got a temperature controlled wine cabinet. The heat is murder on my wine. Murder! Oh, excuse me. I didn't mean to say murder. It's not like my wine killed him!"

She started to sputter with giggles and then struggled to compose her face to counteract her inappropriate remark. Being so close to the detective made her giddy and self-conscious. What must he think of her!

"That's quite alright, Boom Boom. Would you mind showing me your wine collection?"

She was thoroughly confused. He was a beer drinker. Why did he want to see her wine? She didn't know what it was like to be a detective, so she figured he was just being thorough, examining everything that had to do with Bennie. Should she tell him about the money? That might give her motive. She didn't want the nice detective to focus on her.

"This way, Chief. Mind the newspaper."

She led him out to her attached shed and showed him the temperature controlled wine cabinet. It was filled with wine. The detective tugged on latex gloves that magically appeared, opened the door and pulled each one out, reading the label, before sliding it back into its slot.

"I keep it at 56 degrees," she said, watching him

closely. "That's the optimum temperature for Merlot. I don't drink anything else."

"Have you had a bottle recently, Boom Boom?"

"It's been too hot. I do have a Riesling in there for my friend Diddi and a Chardonnay for Josie, but all the rest are Merlot."

"There are eleven bottles of Merlot here, Boom Boom," Varland said, stripping off his gloves and stuffing them into his suit pocket.

"Well, I won't be drinking them alone, I assure you, Chief."

"I thought you just bought a case."

"Mm-hm. It was delivered last week. Why?"

"Because there are only eleven bottles here. I believe a case is twelve."

Boom Boom pulled out the wine individually and examined the labels.

"I'm going to have to call Wine and Such and give them a piece of my mind. You know, when you're my age you have to be so careful, Chief, because people are always trying to rip you off."

"May I take one of these with me, Boom Boom? Perhaps I can acquire a taste."

"Yes, please! Be my guest. I'm going to make a wine drinker out of you yet, Chief Varland." She pulled out one of the bottles and handed it to him. She noticed he used one of the latex gloves to swaddle the bottle. "I've got a sack saver if you want to protect it. My friend Maddie makes them. She uses them to store plastic sacks, but I find they make great wine holders. I just sew up one end."

She led him back into the house and as he waited in the living room, she went to her bedroom and selected a sack saver that had a black background with tan horseshoes. It looked very masculine, just right for the detective. When she returned, he slipped the bottle inside and she drew the strings together around its neck.

"Just a few more questions before I leave. Is that alright, Boom Boom?"

She was a little surprised but figured she was slowly winning him over. She readily agreed but insisted he let her make him something to eat. She had a new recipe for an appetizer. He agreed and sat at the kitchen table, first removing Kissy-poo who had reclaimed the chair. She could feel his eyes on her back. Did he notice her trim figure and how near perfect her rear end still was?

She got out the brick of cream cheese and slapped it on a serving dish. She then opened a jar of jalapeno jelly. She dumped the jelly on top of the cream cheese. She got out a box of special crackers, opened the cellophane and dumped them into a small basket. She laid out two saucers in front of him with a butter knife on each. She filled two glasses with sparkling water and set them on the table. When all was finished, she sat down next to him, her knee touching his.

"Go on," she purred, "eat up."

He looked confused as he picked up the butter knife and a cracker. She did the same and showed him how to slice off a little cream cheese, spread it on the cracker and scoop a little jelly on top. She bit into it.

"Mmm. I saw this at the last block party and thought it looked like something I could do. Good, eh?"

The detective admitted it was and she was thoroughly pleased. He took a drink of the sparkling water, set down the glass and looked her straight in the eyes.

"Did you kill Bennie Uzul, Boom Boom?" he asked.

She blinked in astonishment. "Me! You think I . . . how?"

"Got a rat problem, Boom Boom?"

"What are you talking about, Chief?"

"If I was to look under your sink, would I find any rat poison?"

"Go ahead! I've got nothing to hide!"

He got up from the table, pulled on his latex gloves and began looking under her sink, moving things around. She didn't know what to make of it. He moved from her sink and went down the hallway to the bathroom. She could hear him rummaging around. She heard the back door open and she knew he was now looking in her attached shed. She sighed. The mood was spoiled. She was deeply distressed.

He returned shortly and appeared to tower over her, filling the kitchen with his bulk and testosterone. She could feel blood infuse her face.

"Satisfied?"

"Not quite."

He returned to the table, stripping the gloves from his hands and sat down. He gave her an intense stare that made the blood drain from her face. Her hands felt cold and she trembled all over.

"How much did you hate Bennie Uzul, Boom Boom?"

Her voice was shaky as she tried to answer. "I di-didn't h-hate him. I said I d-di-didn't like him."

"Why not? You two were quite cozy in front of your TV, sipping Merlot, watching the Diamondbacks."

"I d-did at f-first, only n-not . . . later." Her voice was almost a whimper.

"What happened to change that, Boom Boom," he asked, his voice becoming soft and entreating. His face was suddenly gentle and lovely.

"H-he . . . stole from me."

"What did he take from you?"

"B-besides m-my pride and false hopes? He took $8800! Satisfied!"

The detective was kind, reaching over and taking

her ice-cold hands into his big warm ones. "He stole $8,000 from you?"

"No! $8800!" She stood on shaky legs and slammed her palms on the table, making a slapping sound that scared Kissy-poo out of his slumber. "I was saving it to go to the Holy Land. I had it hidden in my lingerie drawer. When I heard he was dead, I knew he stole it. That lousy pestilence was just buttering me up to get at my dough. Now I'll never see where Jesus walked!"

The burst of emotion was too much for her. She slumped into her chair. Kissy-poo jumped onto her lap, purring. She stroked his sleek fur as she spoke.

"I didn't want anyone to know," she sniffed, glancing at the detective. She thought his face looked pained as her words tumbled out. "I was so embarrassed. I used to make fun of the chumps who got scammed, and then for me to fall for a dumb guy just killed my pride. You've got to believe me. I admit I wanted to murder him, but he was already dead. I didn't kill him, Chief Varland. Only after I heard he'd died did I suspect him. I just couldn't believe it; you know what I mean? I just couldn't believe my friend had stolen from me. I just thought I'd misplaced it. I do get forgetful. I was sure I'd find it, but when Madge told us that she'd given him hundreds of dollars and then Maddie said she'd given him $12,000, well, then I knew. I knew!"

The detective did his best to console her. He gave her a tissue and she blew her nose. She wanted him to stay, but in the end he had to leave. He said he would be back, which made her feel better. He left with her bottle of Merlot and she hoped he would find it palatable and come back for more.

Feeling much better, she looked for her tissue to wipe her eyes, but she couldn't find it. She got another one and dabbed her face. She sliced off a wedge of cream cheese and put it on a cracker. Kissy-poo joined her, jumping up on the chair and placing his paws on the table. Boom Boom made up a cracker for him as well and watched as her cat lapped at the cream cheese.

"You know what would go great with this, Kissy-poo?"

"Merow."

"Exactly."

Chapter Fifteen

After he left Boom Boom Klutterbuck, Detective Varland headed for the Forensics Lab to deliver his evidence. The traffic on Hwy 10 West was merciless. He had hit it at the worst possible time, just prior to rush hour. As he sat in traffic, he mulled over his interview. He tried to be objective, but he was strangely attracted to his new suspect. She exuded a kind of incandescent spirit, rare in someone so old. He could imagine her swinging her slender legs around a pole. He laughed to himself at the thought. She was a bit scatter-brained but had all her faculties. He hated himself for making her so unhappy, but it had to be done. If the bottle of wine were the same as the one laced with strychnine that Clement had analyzed, he'd have to arrest her. In his heart, he hoped that it wasn't.

His cell phone rang and he clicked on his Bluetooth. "Varland."

He listened to the startling news and assured the caller he'd follow up. He tapped his steering wheel and requested another number.

"Norm, where you at? Did you meet with that couple? Anything? Nothing. Okay. Write up your report and email it to me. I'm heading over to see Clement. I think there might be a new development. I'll let you know."

The cars in front of him began to move and he slowly eased forward. After a half hour, he took his exit at 7th Avenue. He parked and entered the building.

Dr. Clement was in his office and welcomed him.

"What's new?" the medical examiner asked.

Varland handed over his enshrined bottle of Merlot. Clement raised an eyebrow as he accepted it.

"See if this matches your sample."

"Ah, the delivery system. New suspect?"

"To tell you the truth, I hope not. She's a sweetheart."

"You're getting soft in your old age, Magnus."

Varland smirked and sat across from him. "Maybe so. Any DNA? I'm hoping to charge Mrs. Bradshaw and wrap this up."

"Sorry to have to tell you, but there's no match. She's not the one he was with prior to his death. I put it through the system, but nothing came back as a match. You got any other suspects? This the one?" He waved to the bottle on his desk.

"Damn! I was hoping. Well, try this." He handed a baggie with a tissue in it. "I'm betting it matches."

Clement took it and placed it next to the bottle. "But you don't want it to. She have rat poison?"

"Not that I could find."

"Croquet mallet?"

"Not yet."

"Early days, Magnus, early days. Buck up, old boy. Darkest before the dawn."

After leaving Clement and the Forensic Center, he entered the clogged artery of I-10 East and headed back to Superstition Way Resort. He had one more stop to make before he could clock out and go home. He had visions of a frosty mug of beer, him stretched out on his lounger in t-shirt and shorts watching the Diamondbacks in air-conditioned comfort. The thought made him remember the agonized face of Boom Boom Klutterbuck. This day couldn't be over soon enough.

"Yes, I heard about it," Sandra Fleming countered, glaring at Varland. Her blond hair was recently cut into a short bob, which bounced as she emphasized her words. "So what if I told Gary. I already told the other detective all I know. I haven't a clue why you're here wasting our time."

"You seem a bit defensive, Mrs. Fleming."

"Of course I'm defensive. You've locked up one of my good friends, Detective. Mimi is innocent. She had nothing to do with Bennie's murder."

"I'm only trying to get at the truth, Mrs. Fleming."

"Are you? I think you're railroading her. You've got no evidence. None at all. Zilch!"

"Now, Sandra. Don't get riled," John Fleming urged his wife. "You'll have to forgive my wife, Detective Varland. She's very upset about her friend."

They were seated on the patio of the couple's modular home. It was pleasant there. The carport/patio provided cover from the sun and there was a slight breeze that kept the air moving. It was still over a hundred degrees in the shade.

John Fleming was a tall, rugged individual with a gentle manner. He was dressed in cut-offs and a tank top. He had been gracious and forthcoming. Varland appreciated his protectiveness, but he could see the man had enough muscle that if he felt the need could wield a club with some force. He noticed he had large calloused hands.

His wife, on the other hand, appeared frightened and defensive. He knew Sandra Fleming by sight. She had said she was a former reporter and he assumed she was also observant. If she let down her guard for one moment, he might get some new information. As it was she was sitting with her arms folded across her chest and a frown on her face. He decided to take another tact. He turned to John Fleming.

"Did you know Benito Uzul, Mr. Fleming?"

"Yeah, I knew him. Like I told the other detective, I didn't like him."

"Why?"

"Because he was a jerk."

"How so?"

"I don't know. He was just a nuisance to everyone."

"In what way?"

John Fleming squirmed in his chair. "He got on my nerves."

"Mr. Fleming. I'm investigating a murder. I would appreciate it if you would answer my questions without making me draw the answers out of you."

"I'm sorry, Detective Varland. I didn't want to get involved, but I see I'll have to come clean."

"John!" Sandra Fleming looked apoplectic.

"I'm sorry, Sandra, but we might as well let him know. We've got nothing to be sorry for. The guy was harassing my wife, Detective. They crossed paths a couple of times and he was abusive. I let him know in no uncertain terms that I wouldn't stand for it. You understand, man-to-man, if it had been your wife."

"What did you do to him?"

"Just gave him what he asked for."

"John, please don't," Sandra spoke under her breath.

"And that was . . ." Detective Varland sat forward as John leaned back.

"Just a little beat down. Nothing serious. I knocked him to the ground. When he threatened me and my wife, I might have gotten a little sore and, well, maybe I pushed his face into the ground with my foot. But I sure as hell didn't kill him, Detective!"

"Hm, I see. When was this, Mr. Fleming?"

"A couple days before . . . before he died."

"Tell me everything now and don't leave anything

out," Varland demanded, pulling his notebook from his back pocket and positioning his pen. "I remind you. This is a murder investigation."

John Fleming quickly relayed his confrontation with Bennie Uzul. Varland noticed Sandra was twisting her hands together with anxiety.

"That's all," John swore, placing his hand on his heart.

"Do you own a croquet mallet, Mr. Fleming?"

"I do. I'll go get it," he said, standing.

"Not anymore!" his wife blurted out.

"That's right. Not anymore," John continued, looking askance at his wife, trying to gauge her emotions. "Used to. We're in a league here."

"So the answer is yes. May I see your croquet mallet?"

Sandra jumped from her seat and flung her arms around her husband's waist. "We haven't got it!" she shrieked. "Bennie Uzul stole it!"

"She's right, Detective. I'd forgotten. I don't have it anymore. We're pretty sure Bennie took it that day to get back at me. I was mighty sore about it. It was custom made and I haven't replaced it yet."

"South American Matta wood?" Varland asked, rising from his chair.

John looked taken aback. "How did you know? Sandra got it for me for Christmas last year. It's a beauty. One-of-a-kind. I'd give anything to have it back."

"He didn't do it!" Sandra bawled, rising to her feet. "You can't pin this on him! Bennie stole it! I can swear to it."

"You're not the most credible witness, Mrs. Fleming."

"Do I need a lawyer, Detective Varland?" John asked, looking shocked.

"I can't advise you on that, Mr. Fleming. Do you have any paperwork on your mallet? I'd like to take that."

While John went to get the paperwork, Sandra gave him angry looks.

"He didn't do it," she stated firmly, her eyes blazing.

"I'm not a jury, Mrs. Fleming. I just collect evidence."

"He was killed by John's mallet, wasn't he?"

"I can't say, Mrs. Fleming."

"You don't have to. I can read between the lines. I was a reporter with the *San Jose Courier*. I've got a nose for news and a nose for BS."

"That's quite a nose."

"Don't be smart, Detective Varland. I can tell you're looking for a suspect and John is made to order. You won't believe me, but he's the kindest man I know and he may get riled, but he would never take another's life. He's a Christian, as am I. We're not saints but we follow the teachings of Jesus. John could not, would not, did not kill Bennie Uzul!"

"I appreciate your feelings, Mrs. Fleming. I'm afraid I just follow the evidence."

"You're sure John's croquet mallet killed him?"

"I'm not at liberty to discuss the case. I'm sorry."

"No, you're not! I should have known we wouldn't get justice in a Podunk place like this. I'll call my congressman and alert the media if you arrest him. He's got nothing to do with this. Bennie Uzul was the meanest, most vindictive man I ever met. We can't be the only ones you're investigating."

"I'm sorry, Mrs. Fleming. I can't . . ."

"Talk about the case. I know. Well, I can tell you, there are lots of people who would like to see him dead."

"Like who?"

She seemed a bit flustered at that. He took a step forward and she stepped back, crossing her arms. She looked as if she was ready to bolt, but he knew he had her caught in his piercing gaze.

"Well, Gary Smith for one. I understand he pulled him out of the pool before you even got there. That would make him a suspect, wouldn't it? Why don't you talk to him?"

"I already have. Anyone else?"

She stammered and bit her lip. "I know Maddie Ingersoll lost a bundle to him. Oh, I see you know that. And then, of course, there's Mimi's restraining order, which she had every right to take out on him because he was a creep and was spying on her! And look what you did to her!"

"And don't forget Josie Simone," John said, entering the patio with papers in his hand. He handed them over to Varland and put his arm around his wife.

"John, no!" Sandra hissed, shaking her head like maracas.

"What about Josie Simone?" Varland's eyes glittered under the overhead patio light.

"Well, she was having sex with him. Isn't that right, Sandra? Isn't that what you told me?"

Sandra looked as if her head was going to explode. Detective Varland stepped back, expecting brain matter to start flying.

"Is that right, Mrs. Fleming?"

"Oh, God! Oh, God! Please don't let her know it came from us. Please!"

"Like I said, Mrs. Fleming, I just follow the evidence. Thank you for these, Mr. Fleming. If your mallet happens to turn up, you'll let me know?"

"Of course, Detective."

He put his notebook and pen back in his pocket.

"Have a good evening, folks," he said and walked to his car. He looked back over his shoulder and saw the two in a fierce embrace.

CHAPTER SIXTEEN

When he entered the police station, he relished the cool air. It was six o'clock and the sun was setting, but it was still sweltering outside. He passed by a distraught mother looking for her son and gave a nod to the desk sergeant. He took his coat off as he went down the hallway to the back of the building and entered the homicide room. Detective Rinaldi had clocked out, but Detective Norm Luskowitz was at his desk.

Luskowitz was in his mid-forties, 5'7", barrel-chested, with beefy arms and hands, narrow hips and spindly legs. He sprouted a prominent nose beneath beady brown eyes and above cranberry colored lips that parted to reveal a warm smile as Detective Varland approached. He was genuinely liked by his colleagues, eminently approachable and had an unusual appeal that often caught a suspect off-guard.

"Norm, got a job for you. I need you to pick up Josie Simone for questioning at Superstition Way. Unit #1751."

"Sure, Magnus. I guess you heard we lost the Bradshaw woman. Her lawyer sprung her about an hour ago."

"We won't be charging her. She's been cleared."

"This a new one?"

"Yeah, she has motive and opportunity. All we need is means. Get a warrant to look for rat poison."

"Will do, Chief. What's up? You don't look happy."

"She's our best suspect so far."

"But . . ."

"I don't feel it."

"Your gut again?"

"It's this case, Norm. I can't get a handle on it. I feel like I'm losing my grip. Tell me I'm not."

"Well, if the way you played poker last night is any indication, I'd have to say yes, you're losing it, and you owe me five bucks. What's got you so baffled?"

"These women! They're at my crime scene. They take my witness out from under my nose. They show up when I least expect it. They're every-where I turn. They're covering for each other and giving each other up. One minute I think I'm getting somewhere, and then the next I feel like I'm way off base. It's like I'm spinning in circles. And then there's this Uzul character! What a piece of work. I'd like to say he's just another low-life grifter, preying on the most vulnerable, but he's different; not like anyone I've ever encountered. It's like I have all the blocks but not the capstone. I'm looking for the capstone, Norm."

"I'll admit dealing with these old dears is a bit of a strain, sir. It's like interrogating your own grand-mother. It doesn't feel natural."

"You can say that again. Well, get going. I'm sure her husband will be getting a lawyer as soon as we bring her in."

"I'm on it, sir. Why don't you take a breather? Want me to interrogate her?"

"Maybe that's a good idea. I'm not too objective right now."

He filled in his detective on his interview with the Flemings and felt relief as he watched him leave. Mrs. Simone was another woman from the Superstition Way Aquatics Club. If Luskowitz found poison at her home, he'd wrap up the case. Had he but known what he was getting into, he would have put in his vacation request earlier. He sighed and loosened his belt as he sat in his chair. He pushed it back and put his feet on his desk.

He was baffled. Why?

For one thing, his gut wasn't behind this latest arrest. All the evidence pointed to Josie Simone, but he didn't have the usual "gotcha" feeling when he had a suspect picked up.

For another thing, his victim Bennie Uzul, aka Benito Uzul, aka Benito Ordaz, was all wrong. The guy had too many aliases and had covered his tracks for something bigger than a $20,000 score from an old woman. He sat up, dropping his feet to the floor and began searching through the paperwork. Not finding what he was looking for, he spun in his seat and logged onto his computer.

The CSU had emailed their report on the items from Bennie Uzul's car. It only confirmed what he had suspected earlier. Bennie was planning to leave, but not in any normal way. He had planned a methodical escape, one in which he could disappear completely—possibly for years. There was one item that piqued his interest. He picked up the phone.

"This is Detective Varland. I want Benito Uzul's laptop brought over for Detective Garza to examine—as soon as possible. Good. Yes, I was just looking at it. No, I didn't. Something I should know? Yeah, send that over, too. Thanks."

He hung up and stared at the computer screen. He clicked on the attachment connected to the Crime Scene Unit's list. It opened to reveal an additional list of the items in Bennie's file bin and the metal lock box.

The file bin had a treasure trove of information on Bennie's movements over the years. There were several bank statements from four different banks. He'd have Garza check them out, but it appeared Bennie had sizeable accounts in four different states. There was also a scrapbook filled with photos of Bennie with different women, mostly from Las Vegas. According to the report, one woman appeared in more than a few of the photos and was identified in one as Moogie. The CSU was going to send it over with the laptop.

The information on Bennie's lock box sent his gut into a nosedive. He had three different passports, one issued by the U.S. for Benito Uzul, one issued by Venezuela for Benito Ordaz and a third issued by the Ukraine for Sergei Voronkov. Another alias!

He wiped his forehead. This was beginning to smell like organized crime. What was he supposed to do with this information? The lock box also contained a Makarov PM, a Russian semi-automatic pistol used by the Russian military. Bennie was one deep character. He closed the email and stared at the screen, running through different scenarios that would help him make sense of all the information.

He located an email from Detective Garza with an attachment. He clicked on the attachment and immediately printed it out. He took the printout to the break room, poured some acidic leftover coffee into a mug, adding lots of creamer, and sat down to examine it thoroughly. The information was startling. He made notations as he read.

Bennie Uzul, aka Benito Ordaz, was actually born in Venezuela in 1945. In 1956, he and his parents, Darla and Joseph Ordaz, immigrated to the US and settled in Oakland, California. Mr. Ordaz worked as a used car salesman and his wife as a housekeeper. Much to Varland's surprise, Benito Ordaz excelled in school and received an academic scholarship to San Francisco State. He graduated Magna Cum Laude with a Bachelor of Science in accounting. No dummy there. In 1968, he worked in the accounting department at

Brittania Advertising. (That confirmed Bella Adler's story.) He was terminated in 1970. No reason given.

Nothing on him after that until 1973 when he was caught shoplifting twice at the same department store and arrested. He had stolen the same item both times. It was a "best friends forever" water globe. Because of the unusual theft, his stellar academic career and an impassioned plea for leniency from his parents, the court had ordered him into counseling. It was at the Breaking Barriers Counseling Center in Oakland that he had met Mimi Bradshaw, aka Minuet O'Malley.

After he completed his court ordered six-week counseling stint, he left California and did a number of odd jobs across the United States; at least the ones that he'd stayed at long enough to have a W-2 on file. He had two outstanding warrants for theft, one in Oklahoma, and one in Illinois. He ended up in Washington DC in 1974, where he was caught pirating the new video game, Pong, and was sentenced to two years. Inexplicably, his sentence was commuted and his warrants were expunged. After that, he disappeared for twenty years.

The next time he surfaced was in 1995 under his new name: Benito Uzul, when he'd received a new passport and purchased a mobile home unit at Costa del Grande in Arizona. That was the end of the report.

Where had he been for those twenty years? Why had his sentence been commuted? Who could possibly expunge outstanding warrants in two states? There was only one answer.

Detective Luskowitz entered the break room and interrupted his musings.

"She's in Room Two, sir. Want to observe?"

Varland groaned as he rose to his feet and followed Luskowitz to Interrogation Room Two. He went into the viewing room where he could observe behind one-way glass. Josie Simone sat hunched in the chair with her hands folded in front of her on the table. She was an attractive, petite woman in her seventies with light brown hair, streaked with blond, cut just below her chin. She straightened as Luskowitz entered the room. He now remembered her from Mrs. Sheridan's house. She was one of those women from the Aquatics Club.

He flipped on the receiver to listen.

"Do you know why you're here, Mrs. Simone?" Detective Luskowitz said in a conversational tone.

"No. I have no idea."

"We need your help. You see, a man's dead. We need to find his killer. We think you might know something we don't."

"I'm sure I don't."

"But you do want to help us out, don't you?" Luskowitz purred, his voice rumbling like a foot massager.

"Of course, but I don't know how I can."

"You can be honest with me, Mrs. Simone. Don't let things prey on your mind. Just tell us the truth."

"I have been honest. I don't know anything."

"Oh, I think you do," he said, his voice rumbling low and dangerous. He bent over the table and looked sideways at her. "We know all about you and Bennie Uzul. You two were quite intimate. Isn't that right?"

Varland watched the color drain from her face. She bent her head to rest her forehead on the table. Her shoulders began to shake as she tried not to cry. Luskowitz turned to look at Varland with a 'how far do you want me to go?' look.

He turned back to the woman and slammed his palms on the table, making it rattle with a loud clang. Josie jumped and looked alarmed.

"You had sex with him!"

"What!" she cried out, alarmed.

"Admit it. He was your lover."

Yes," she whispered. "I guess he was."

Detective Luskowitz backed off. "You're married, aren't you?"

"You know I am. You met my husband."

"Did Mr. Simone know about you and Bennie?"

"David knows nothing. I made sure of that!" That got her fired up. She appeared to be collecting herself. She straightened her shoulders and looked the detective in the eyes. "We were very discreet. If you must know, we met in the Laundromat, early in the morning, between security shifts. No one knew, especially not David. How do you know about us? Nobody did."

"You and your husband having marital problems?" Luskowitz ignored her question and began circling her.

"We are happily married," she asserted, turning her head to follow his movement. The knuckles on her folded hands turned white. "This, this thing I did with Bennie, had nothing to do with my marriage."

"I bet David would disagree."

"Yes, he would," she moaned, rubbing her temples with shaking fingertips. "I don't know how to make you understand this, Detective, but Bennie meant nothing to me. He was just . . . just a diversion, maybe even a way to get back at David. I don't know. You see, I wanted to go to Rome for our fortieth anniversary, but David wanted to stay home and have the kids visit. After forty years, I expected something . . . well, exciting. I was hoping Rome would renew our . . . our—let's call it passion. Is that too much to ask? Oh, I don't know why I did it! I love David very much."

"So you took up with Bennie for a thrill ride. Is that it?"

Varland could see a hint of a smile on her lips as if she were recalling something sweet. The forbidden fruit, perhaps.

"That's a good way of putting it," she replied softly. "It was thrilling. Not the sex, that was just okay, but the fear of being discovered, that was thrilling. The thrill of being bad. You know what I mean? Can you understand that?"

"Did you kill him?" he shouted, slamming his hands on the table in front of her.

She flinched and her eyes widened in shock. "No! Why would I? I was enjoying myself. He was, too. I had no reason to kill him. He was leaving anyway. He said it was over, and I was a little relieved to be honest. I was . . . becoming . . . addicted. I kept trying to stop, but I couldn't. It was wrong. So wrong! I'm sorry that he's dead. He was good to me. I don't know who killed him, but it wasn't me."

"You say he was leaving? Where was he going?"

"I don't know. He just said it was over."

"Tell me exactly. What did he say?"

"He said this was his farewell performance but that he would give me the spin of my life." She lowered her chin and muffled a chuckle with her hand, coughed and looked up innocently at Detective Luskowitz.

At that moment, Detective Varland saw a young, desirable woman, radiating sexuality and then just as suddenly a woman past her prime, cheeks sagging, worry lines at her eyes and across her brow. It was a disconcerting moment for him.

He was past his prime. His mother constantly nagged him about being single and childless. She didn't count Victoria, his first wife, as she had failed to produce. It had been five years since his divorce. He was now sixty years old, too old to start a family, getting a little soft around the middle. Only ten more years and he would be like this woman, seeking sexual thrills with a loser in a Laundromat. The idea horrified him. He vowed to turn his life around. He would do as his mother asked and sign up for one of those online dating services. As soon as he made the vow, he knew he would not keep it. However, the fact remained that he was lonely—no one to make guacamole for his friends.

He shook his shoulders and stretched, stifling a yawn and refocused on the interview. Josie was looking older and more tired. Norm was just getting started.

"How did that make you feel?"

"Relieved."

"You didn't feel the least bit rejected? Come on, don't take me for a fool."

"Maybe a little. I wasn't prepared for it. It came as a surprise."

"Come on, it made you mad."

"I wasn't mad."

"Yes, you were. Admit it! You were furious. He was leaving and the thrill ride was over."

"I wasn't. I was just surprised. It was a relief."

"Didn't you just say you were addicted to the sex?"

"Uh, did I? I guess so."

"You know what addicts do when they can't get a fix, Mrs. Simone?"

"No."

"Anything! They lie, steal, and even kill! Did you murder him because you couldn't get your fix, Josie?"

"No! I didn't do it!"

Luskowitz backed off again. He was a seasoned interrogator and was at his best. He would win her confidence, then slam her with the facts, then back off and do it all over again. He was slowly whittling her down to the breaking point.

"His death must have been very hard on you."

"I was shocked. I can't imagine who would kill him."

"When did you see him last?"

"Four-twenty, Wednesday morning."

"You're very sure of the time, Mrs. Simone."

She colored ever so slightly and placed her hands on her cheeks. "I left right after the spin cycle was done."

"Excuse me?"

"This is extremely embarrassing, Detective Luskowitz. I'd rather not say any more than that, but trust me, when the spin cycle was done at 4:15, I got dressed and left Bennie in the Laundromat—and he was very much alive."

"Did he get dressed, uhm, after the spin cycle was done?"

"He was doing his yoga poses like he always does. He gave me a kiss and slapped my bottom and sent me on my way! I always left right . . . after. He always stretched afterward, but I don't know how long. I never stayed. When I left him, he was doing a tree pose. That's all I know."

"Was he naked?"

"Oh, you're so mean!" Her temper flared and her cheeks burned. "He was in his boxer shorts."

"Where were the rest of his clothes?"

"How should I know, on the floor, on one of the washers, all over, I don't know. I wasn't interested in that. We were done and I had to get home before David woke up."

"Did anyone see you? Can anyone vouch for the time you left?"

"N-not that I saw. Why? Was someone else there? Someone saw us? Who? Oh, my god! Please tell me no one saw us!"

"Please sit down, Mrs. Simone. Did you meet anyone on the way out?"

"N-no. N-no one."

"You don't seem as sure about that. I can only help you, Mrs. Simone, if you tell me everything."

"I'm sure it's nothing. I didn't see anyone, but I did hear something, something odd."

"What did you hear?"

"Well, at first I thought it was one of the bunnies; they're all over the place. Kind of a rustling sound, but then I heard something else; like a clicking sound, like plastic clicking. I'm not describing it right. I stopped and listened, but I didn't hear anything more."

"A clinking sound like plastic. Hmm. What did you make of it?"

"Nothing. I only just thought of it now because you're badgering me. Probably the same person *you* say saw us. Probably the killer! You're wasting your time. I admit I'm a terrible woman, an adulteress, but I'm not a murderer! I'd like to go home now, Detective Luskowitz. I've answered your questions and I've been patient while you've grilled me when I should be home with my husband who is probably out of his mind with worry and suspicion. Oh! After how careful I've been. You've ruined everything!"

"Mrs. Simone, your DNA was on the victim's clothes, which makes you the last person to have seen him alive. Which makes you our prime suspect."

Her face blanched and she looked as if she were going to faint. Detective Luskowitz had his face right next to hers. She winced.

"No, I'm not," she said in a modulated tone of certainty. She turned her face and was nearly nose-to-nose with the detective. "The last person to see him alive was the killer. Not me. I did not kill him. I want a lawyer. Right now! I'm not saying another word." She crossed her arms and pressed her lips together.

Detective Luskowitz turned to the glass and raised an eyebrow.

"I'll be back in a minute, Mrs. Simone. Sit tight."

Varland watched as Norm left the room. Josie crossed her arms on the table, rested her head on them and her shoulders began to shake.

Detective Luskowitz entered the viewing room. He stood next to Varland and stared at the forlorn woman at the table. He wiped his brow and exhaled in a whoosh.

"Man, that was brutal. I feel like I've just whipped my Aunt Ursula. Kind of reminds me of her. What do you think?"

"Not feeling it."

"Me neither. Got to admit I have a hard time believing she was shagging that bastard Uzul. Kind of gives me a new perspective on getting old."

Varland chuckled. "I know what you mean."

"Should we let her go?"

"Nice touch with the DNA. I think you're right there, but we won't know until Clement can compare them. Get that and then we'll let her go."

Luskowitz left the room and Varland watched as he entered the interrogation room with a plastic cup of water.

"Here you go, ma'am."

He set the glass in front of her. She picked it up and smiled gratefully, if not a little warily, at him. She took a small sip and then drained the glass. She set it down on the table.

"We appreciate you answering our questions. I hope you realize that we're just being thorough."

"I can go?"

"Yes, ma'am. I'll have Officer Frey take you home."

"Am I still a suspect?"

"Yes, ma'am. If you think of anything else about that sound you heard, please call us. It might have been the killer. It might eliminate you as a suspect."

"I can go?"

"Yes, ma'am. Come this way. We'll get you home quick as a wink."

"And you won't tell David? About me and Bennie, I mean."

"No need to, ma'am. You can tell him whatever you like about why we brought you in. Of course, if we have to charge you and there's a trial, it will come out. I can't advise you, but if I were your husband, I'd want to know beforehand. This way, ma'am."

She picked up the plastic glass on the table and started to follow him out.

"You can leave that here," Detective Luskowitz said.

She nodded and dropped it into the wastebasket.

CHAPTER SEVENTEEN

Eight o'clock on the dot, the ladies of the Superstition Aquatics Club came into the courtyard and began arranging their chairs around a table. Madge brought Styrofoam cups filled with coffee and Diddi set down a box of breakfast pastries.

Babe was first to sit. She was eager to begin but didn't say a word. Madge and Diddi quickly imitated her. Sandra, looking sleepy and uncommunicative, pulled out a chair and sat. She had dark circles under her eyes. Maddie, Margarita and Cicie joined her, each glancing at Babe to see if she was ready to begin. When it looked as if she wasn't, Maddie opened the box of pastries and began dispensing them on small cafe plates that she pulled from her pink polka-dotted sack saver.

Sweets was next to arrive, dressed in tight jeans and a denim jacket with her motorcycle helmet under her arm. She sat and put her helmet under the chair. She snagged a pastry and bit into it. She let out of sigh of pleasure.

"I don't know how you can be dressed like that," Cicie said to Sweets. "Aren't you sweating?"

"Nah. I'm always cold and when I'm on my bike I just freeze."

At that moment, Veronica rushed in, breathless, as if she were bursting with news.

"I'm not late, am I?"

She quickly took a seat next to Cicie. Loretta sat next to Babe and whispered something in her ear. Babe nodded but pressed her lips together. Boom Boom was unusually quiet, sipping her coffee and staring at the edge of the table.

When Mimi walked in with Bella, her red hair gleaming in the morning light, all the ladies shouted their greetings. Cicie and Loretta got up and hugged her. Cicie pulled her to a chair beside hers. Bella sat, looking pleased. Maddie passed over two plates of pastries.

"You poor thing. Was it just awful?" Margarita asked.

"Worst experience of my life," Mimi answered, smiling bravely.

"They let you go. That's good," Sweets added, wiping her lip.

"I'm not sure what happens next. They didn't charge me; they just held me for questioning. I'm so embarrassed. What must you think of me? My reputation's ruined."

"No it's not, honey," Madge said, patting her shoulder. "We squashed any gossip. If anyone asked, we just said you were helping the police with their investigation. No one knows but us."

"Thank you," Mimi said, brushing away sudden tears, looking around the table. "Where's Josie?"

"She knew we were meeting this morning," Babe said firmly, finally opening her mouth. "We're not waiting for her. I'm calling the meeting of the Superstition Aquatics Club to order. First, let's thank Diddi for the pastries."

Diddi acknowledged their thanks with a nod of her head, but she looked pained. She pressed a hand to her abdomen and her smile was tight.

"Are you feeling alright, dear?" Maddie asked, her face full of concern.

"Just indigestion. Don't mother me, Maddie!"

"Don't bark at me," Maddie shot back. "I was only asking."

"Second, we want to welcome Mimi back. We're so happy you're here, dear. We were so worried."

"I'm glad to be here," Mimi acknowledged gratefully. "I missed you."

"Now, to business," Babe commanded. "Sandra, you wanted this meeting. You have the floor."

They all looked at Sandra, but to everyone's amazement, she shook her head no. Babe wasn't sure what to do. She had news but wanted to spring it on everyone when the opportunity presented itself.

"Diddi?"

"What?"

"Bella?"

"Not me."

"Madge?"

"Uh-uh."

"For god's sake," Babe fumed, "what's wrong with everyone?"

"I have something to say," Veronica said, waving her hand.

"The chair recognizes Veronica," Babe said.

"I thought we were going to be called the Superstition Murder Club."

"That's right!" Sweets concurred.

"No, we're not. We never voted on it," Babe said hotly.

"Let's vote!" Veronica exclaimed. "All in favor?"

Everyone but Babe raised a hand. Reluctantly, she joined them, waving her hand dismissively.

"In that case, I am no longer chair. I turn it over to . . ." She looked around the table. "Cicie."

Cicie was startled. "Me? Are you sure, Babe?" Seeing that she was, she said, "Okay. Uh-hm. Let the Superstition Murder Club come to order. We are here to find out who killed Bennie Uzul so we can get back into the pool. I don't want another day to go by without our class!"

The ladies all nodded sadly. Their daily aerobics at the pool were necessary for their wellbeing. Although it was not particularly rigorous, the non-weight-bearing exercises kept their joints from stiffening up and many credited it for keeping them limber, flexible and alive. As many of them were widows, the social interaction gave them a sense of belonging and the discipline gave them a sense of accomplishment.

"When I call on you, I want you to give your report," Cicie continued.

"Nicely done, Cicie," Sweets grinned. "You almost sounded like Babe, except you forgot the accent."

"Ve vill begin vit the sveetest among us," Cicie intoned in her best German accent. Her smile faded when she saw Babe glaring at her. She gulped. "Go ahead, Loretta."

"I spoke with Regina in the office. Detective Varland talked to Linda yesterday. I found out there were two complaints about Bennie. One was from Mrs. Greenfeld because he swore at Patton, and the other was from Jim Cantor and David Simone!"

"Josie's husband!" Cicie exclaimed.

"Patton isn't Josie's husband. He's Greta's Schnauzer," Maddie contended. "Even I know that."

Loretta smiled indulgently. "No, Maddie. Josie's husband made a complaint that Bennie was parking in front of his house."

"Oh, boy," Sweets said, wide-eyed. "That's not good. What a schmuck. I'm sure that made things awkward for Josie. I can't imagine that conversation."

"Is that why she's not here?" Veronica asked.

"He also asked about the resort," Loretta said.

"He took a list of all the properties available. Do you think he's planning to move here?"

"Who knows how a detective thinks," Sweets shrugged. "Is that it?"

"No. He asked all kinds of questions about the Croquet League."

Sandra spit coffee on the table and began coughing. Cicie slapped her on the back until she recovered. Maddie mopped up the spots of coffee.

"You okay?" Sweets asked. Sandra nodded mutely and averted her eyes.

"Go on, Loretta," Babe encouraged.

"That's about it. To be honest, I was surprised I got that much. Why was he asking about croquet? You and John are in the league, aren't you, Sandra?"

All eyes turned to her. Her face was like a thundercloud, dark and foreboding. It broke with a thunderclap.

"He thinks John killed Bennie!" she wailed, burying her face in her hands.

"Oh, Sandra!" Cicie cried, "That can't be true!"

"Why hasn't he been arrested, then?" Sweets inquired, taking a bite of pastry and daintily dabbing her mouth with a napkin, completely oblivious of the impact of her words. "He must not have the evidence. Or is he going to arrest you, too? I guess you both could have killed him."

"Sweets! You're out of order," Babe barked, giving

Cicie a look. "Go on, Sandra. You have the floor. Pay no attention to Sweets."

"He came over all nice and friendly, and then bam! He hit us with a demand to see John's croquet mallet. Remember, I told you Bennie stole it. We told him that, but I don't think he believed us! I think . . . that he thinks . . . that John killed him with his croquet mallet! Oh!" She dissolved into tears. Maddie quickly pulled more tissues from her sack saver. The ladies passed them to Sandra who took them and mutely nodded through her tears.

"That's ridiculous!" Margarita cried. "John has an alibi."

Sandra looked up, startled. "What?"

"His alibi," Margarita reminded her. "You said he was playing tennis at the time of the murder."

"That's right! He was! There are plenty of witnesses who can say he was there. Oh, Margarita, you saved us!"

Margarita looked a little shocked, but with the smiling nods of her companions, she felt like she was among friends and decided to confess.

"I went out with Bennie!" she blurted. "I didn't want to say anything before because of Josie, but it's true. I . . . I went dancing with him."

"Good for you, Margarita!" Sweets inserted in defiance of Babe's rules of order. "It's about time you got out and enjoyed yourself. You did enjoy yourself, didn't you? I mean we all know he was a louse, but you did have fun, didn't you?"

"It was the most wonderful night I've had in a long time," Margarita confessed. "I didn't know how much I was missing the nightlife. Since . . ."

"We know," Maddie consoled. "Widowhood is not for the faint of heart."

"Out of order," Babe intoned. "Cicie, Margarita is out of order. You have to call on her first."

"Sorry, Babe. I recognize Margarita."

"I'm done. I just hope you guys can forgive me," Margarita pleaded.

"Nothing to forgive. I'm proud of you for sharing," Loretta said gently, patting Margarita's shoulder. "You know you're among friends." She had privately counseled her and knew Margarita had been very depressed since her husband's death.

"But that's not right," Bella argued. She had red discolorations on her cheeks that appeared to be growing. "Tell them the whole story, Margarita."

"I don't know what you mean, Bella."

"Yes, you do. He assaulted you."

"What!" all the ladies said at once. There was a flurry of consolation and angry retorts until Babe banged on the table with the flat of her hand.

"Order!" Babe shouted, eyeing Cicie. "Margarita has the floor."

"Oops, that's right. Order! Margarita has the floor," Cicie announced.

Everyone looked expectantly and sympathetically at Margarita.

"But I . . . wasn't assaulted."

"Of course you were," Bella chided. "You practically told me as much."

"No, I wasn't, Bella! He was a perfect gentleman."

"That can't be," Bella maintained. "You said he assaulted you."

"No, I didn't. Where did you get that?"

"You said he assaulted you and you felt like 'old pitiful Margarita' again."

"I never!" Margarita countered, standing up. Cicie pulled her back down.

"Looks like you got it wrong, Bella," Sweets pointed out. "I think Margarita had a pretty good time with our friend Bennie. Didn't you?"

"I know what you're all thinking, but I don't care. He took me dancing and . . . and we kissed at the door . . . but that's it. I'm not ashamed to say it. I liked it."

"But you were so angry," Bella argued, embarrassed, trying to make sense of things. "I just thought . . ."

"That I had sex with him? Well, I didn't. I wanted to, but he didn't make a move. That's what I was angry about, that and I'd just learned he was sleeping with Josie at the same time he took me dancing!"

"Why did you think she'd been assaulted, Bella?" Loretta asked, turning to give Bella her famous stare. One could never resist Loretta's stare.

Now it was Bella's turn to be on the hot seat. She squirmed, her cheeks flamed, but she finally confessed.

"Because fifty years ago he assaulted me. Oh, let's not put any gloss on it! He raped me."

"Bella!"

"Oh, my god!"

"I'll kill him!" This came from Diddi; only it came out sounding like "I killed him!" She looked all of her ninety-five years, pale and drawn, but her eyes were fiery darts.

That stopped everyone from talking as they stared at her, but seeing she didn't mean it, they quickly returned their attention to Bella.

"Oh, Bella, what a terrible secret to keep," Margarita moaned, getting up and hugging her friend. "I never knew."

"I hate him even more," Mimi growled, "I wish I had killed him!"

"Me, too!" Veronica snarled.

"Girls! Don't say that!" Madge gasped, alarmed.

"I'm sorry, Madge," Veronica said, feeling guilty.

"Okay, I take it back," Mimi grumbled. "He was a despicable man, but he didn't deserve to die—maybe castrated. Go on, Bella."

"I never told anyone. I thought if I never said anything, then it wouldn't have happened. But it did. I've
been thinking about it since yesterday. It all came
back in a rush after that detective questioned me. In
retrospect, I probably should have had some counseling at the time. I've tried to forget. I was so angry
with myself that I let it happen. I was used to being
in control."

"You weren't to blame," Loretta declared. Her
eyes flashed with righteous anger. "It wasn't your
fault. Repeat that! Say it, Bella."

"It wasn't my fault."

"Again. Louder."

"It wasn't my fault!" Bella stood up and yelled,
raising her arms.

The ladies applauded as Bella collapsed on her
chair.

"Loretta, you're glowing!" Boom Boom whispered
loudly. Everyone followed her gaze. A white sheen
of light glowed all around Loretta. Everyone gasped.
The sheen vanished as a cloud passed over the sun,
but Loretta had an aura of righteous indignation that
was undeniable.

"If you want to talk about it privately, Bella, I'm
here for you."

"Thank you, Loretta. Sorry, Margarita. I got it all
wrong. Forgive me?"

"Of course! Why, if not for you, Bella, I wouldn't

have met Bay. You remember the man at Bugsy's? The one with the dance studio?"

"You're seeing him?"

"Twice already."

"Is this serious?"

Margarita laughed. "I don't know. I'm just having fun."

"That's good. That's good," Sweets nodded.

"Out of order, Sweets. I recognize Veronica." Cicie arched her eyebrows at Babe, who gave her a satisfied smile.

Veronica scooted her chair forward and it screeched on the concrete. She bent in and everyone followed suit.

"I talked to my friend in the police department. Get this. Bennie didn't die from drowning."

"I know that," Sweets smirked. "It was a blow to the head."

"You're out of order again, Sweets," Cicie chided. Sweets grinned and shrugged.

"No, it wasn't. He was poisoned! With rat poison."

"Rat poison!" Boom Boom woke up and looked terrified.

"Poison!" Loretta blanched. "Are you sure?"

"Not with a croquet mallet?" Sandra asked, her eyes gleaming with hope.

"Not with a croquet mallet. Rat poison," Veronica reaffirmed, smiling broadly.

"Put a fork in me, girls, I'm done!" Boom Boom wailed.

"What are you talking about, Boom Boom?" Maddie asked, looking confused. "It's okay to use your fingers. I am."

"Chief Varland was at my house yesterday," Boom Boom continued, ignoring Maddie. "He asked me if I had mice. I thought he was making fun of Kissy-poo. Like he wasn't a good mouser or something. Dumb, dumb, dumb!"

"Out of order, Boom Boom," Cicie reminded her. "Veronica has the floor."

"Shut up, Cicie!" Sweets demanded.

"I yield the floor to Boom Boom," Veronica replied excitedly.

All eyes turned to Boom Boom. She scrunched her face up until she looked like a shrunken apple doll.

"I take the fifth!"

"You can't do that!" Sweets laughed. "That's only in court. Out with it."

"You *did* meet with him, then," Veronica accused. "I told you to be careful. You shouldn't mess around with a murder investigation, Boom Boom."

"Call me Gertrude," Boom Boom wailed. "I got suckered!"

"I recognize Boom . . . Ger . . . oh, what the heck. Spill it," Cicie said with exasperation.

"I thought he wanted to taste my wine, but he obviously had other motives."

"That's okay, Boom Boom. We've all been fooled by men," Mimi admitted. "How else does the species continue."

"I gave him a bottle of my wine. I wondered why he picked it up with rubber gloves. I was so blasted stupid I even thought he'd go home, open it and find it was so delicious that he'd call me and set up a date to have more. Dumb, dumb, dumb!"

"I don't understand," Maddie stated. "You wanted him to pay for it?"

"No, Maddie, he wanted my fingerprints! I think he suspects me!"

"You're right," Veronica inserted, looking askance at Cicie who was about to say something, but then closed her mouth. "From what my friend says, the poison was put in a glass of wine. In *Merlot*," Veronica said.

"Oh, my god! Oh, my god! I'm going to jail!" Boom Boom cried, standing up and flapping her arms like she hoped to fly away. "I'm too old to go to jail! I don't want to die in jail! Oh, what am I going to do? What am I going to do?"

"Oh, Boom Boom!" Cicie cried, standing up and embracing her friend.

"Calm yourself, Boom Boom!" Loretta shouted. "No one's going to arrest you!"

Boom Boom looked at Loretta, as she and Cicie sat back down. "Are you sure?"

"You have nothing to worry about," Mimi inserted into the general buzz of exclamations and murmurs. "I'm their number one suspect."

"No, I am," Maddie said proudly. "Maxwell told me so."

"Don't forget, I gave him money, too," Madge added, "but the detective hasn't been to see me yet. I'm more worried about Reverend Julian. He was furious when he found out that Bennie was a con man. He was counting on his donation."

"Really, Madge! He's a man of God," Loretta admonished.

"The root of all evil is money," Sweets teased.

"The love of money is the root of all evil," Loretta corrected.

"Wouldn't be the first preacher to fall off the holy wagon," Sweets argued. "I'd say he's a suspect."

"Cicie!" Babe shouted.

Cicie jerked, dropped her pastry and pounded her hand on the table. "Order! Now where were we? Oh, yes. Who hasn't given their report?"

"Me," Sweets said, raising her hand. "I talked to Gary. He admitted he pulled the body from the pool. That detective was sure pissed. Gary said Bennie was a pervert."

"Herbert who?"

"Pervert, Maddie. He thought Bennie was a pervert! He found him in the Laundromat in his boxer shorts."

"First you think he's a Peeping Tom and now a pervert. He wasn't anything like that. He was a gentleman."

"A gentleman creep," Sweets smirked. "Gary didn't know anything about him stealing, but he had some stories to tell about him hitting on the women at the pool. That guy sure got around. Any one of them could have murdered him."

"Like who?" Sandra asked. "Any of them suspects?"

Veronica lowered her voice and looked around. "Rosie Davidson, Melanie Yaeger, and Cheryl Fortesque. Those are the only ones Gary could remember."

"We've got to interrogate them!" Sandra pounced on the news. "Immediately!"

"Listen to this!" Sweets interrupted. "He said Bennie's head was split open."

"How horrible!" Margarita cried. "Poor Bennie!" She looked around at the faces and swallowed. "I mean it is horrible, right?"

"Tragic," Madge said, shaking her head sadly.

"Veronica said it was rat poison that killed him," Mimi reminded them.

"In my Merlot!" Boom Boom moaned. "Oooh! I feel sick."

"Then there might be more than one killer," Sandra rallied. "This is the best news I've heard all week!"

"Great job, Sweets. Are you finished?" Cicie asked.

"No. There's more. Check this out. You won't believe it. Gary had a motive, too. He hated Bennie with a passion."

"Why?" Mimi asked. "What did he have against Bennie?"

"Moogie."

"Margaret Googin! What does she have to do with it?" Madge asked.

"Hey, I'm just telling you what Gary told me. He had a thing going with her and then along comes Bennie and all of a sudden he's yesterday's news. I can't believe he was dating her. I thought he had better taste. If you ask me, Moogie and Bennie were made for each other. I'll just bet she killed him."

"We all know you can't stand her, Sweets," Bella remarked, "but that's no reason to accuse her of murder."

"Oh, come on," Sweets argued, "you know she's a royal b-i-t-c-h. How many times has she given us a hard time about our class? Don't forget she also reported me because she didn't like the sound of my motorcycle? She should go to the top of our list."

"Is anyone keeping a list?" Cicie asked.

"I am," Veronica piped up. She pulled out her cell

phone and typed in Moogie's name. "Should I put Gary on the list, too?"

"Add him," Cicie nodded.

"What about those other three?"

"Add them," Cicie replied.

"I know Rosie Davidson," Mimi said, "but I doubt she'd kill him."

"I can talk to Melanie. She's in my glassworking class," Bella said, nodding.

"That leaves Cheryl Fortesque and Moogie," Veronica said.

"Cheryl's already left for the season," Cicie said. "That leaves Moogie."

"If it's all the same to you, I'll investigate Moogie," Sweets volunteered.

"I'm not so sure that's a good idea, Sweets. You only want to push her buttons and get into her face," Bella argued.

"I'll take Loretta with me. How's that? How 'bout it, Loretta?"

"I'm not sure I'd be any more objective. She tried to get my Bible study banned. She said it discriminated against atheists. I had to ask forgiveness for my bad thoughts."

"Please, Loretta," Sweets begged. "If anything, you could exonerate her and appease your conscience."

"You have a point, Sweets. Okay, let's do it later this afternoon."

"Mimi and Bella, find out what you can from Rosie and Melanie. Who else has a report?" Cicie looked around the table. Maddie was waving her hand. "I recognize Maddie."

"Diddi and I talked to Laura in the Activities Office," Maddie announced. "Tell them, Diddi."

Diddi cleared her throat and leaned back. "First I just want to say, don't worry, Boom Boom. If he suspected you of murder, you would be in jail right now. He's just collecting evidence. He's got diddly-squat!"

Before Babe could say anything, Cicie shouted, "I recognize Diddi!"

Diddi looked at her with forbearance. She straightened her crisp, white blouse and rubbed her hands on her slacks.

"The only thing we found out was that Bennie was being a pest, as usual. He wanted Laura to hire him as a driver. She asked for references and he didn't have any. He threatened her with, how did she say it, Maddie?"

"What?"

"Never mind. He said he'd make her sorry. He left before Security got there."

"Laura did it!" Maddie exclaimed. "Put her on the list!"

"She did not, Maddie." Diddi fumed.

"Then who?"

"Is that all you got?" Sweets scoffed.

"That's all," Diddi replied.

"You're out of order again, Sweets. Anyone else have a report? No one?"

"I do," Babe smiled broadly. "Cicie recognize me."

"Go ahead, Babe. Oh, all right! I recognize Babe."

"My daughter's here! I just called her in DC yesterday and this morning she walked in the door. Can you believe that? I told her what's been going on. She's going to talk to that detective for us."

"What can she do?" Veronica asked, puzzled.

"She's Secret Service. She can do anything," Babe said proudly.

That appeared to satisfy everyone.

"More coffee?" Madge asked. She collected empty cups and went to refill them from the coffee urn. Before she returned, a phone began ringing. Several ladies began checking their cell phones. Babe was not amused.

"Whoever's phone that is, you're supposed to mute it when . . ."

"Out of order!" Cicie pointed at her, triumphantly.

"Sorry, Babe. It's mine," Veronica admitted, chagrined. She got up and moved out of hearing range.

Madge returned with the coffee and everyone took a cup. Diddi started the box of pastries around the circle again.

They were just biting into their second helping

of breakfast pastries when Veronica came running back, her eyes wide and her hands flapping.

"Josie's been arrested! For murder!"

CHAPTER EIGHTEEN

The startling news broke up the meeting. Maddie and Diddi left quickly. Maddie appeared close to fainting and Diddi looked a sickly shade of green. Madge was close behind them, saying she needed to be alone. Mimi broke down in tears and ran to her car. Sandra was close on her heels, saying that she needed to talk to John. Sweets and Loretta decided to track Moogie down right away and see if they should bring her to Detective Varland's attention. The rest of the ladies decided to go to breakfast and make a plan on how to get Josie out of jail.

"Now, if she's home, you let me do the talking," Loretta admonished, stopping Sweets in front of the door of Unit #1000.

"You'll be too nice and we won't get any information out of her," Sweets argued. "Let's do the good cop, bad cop routine. I'll be aggressive and rude, and then you come in all sweet and nice and gain her confidence. That's the way to do it."

"I don't know," Loretta winced. "I'd rather we just be ourselves."

"Like I said, good cop, bad cop. Hey, look at this!" Sweets said, pointing with her toe at three little brown rectangles near the doorway.

"What is it?" Loretta asked, looking over Sweets' shoulder.

Sweets dug into her pocket and pulled out a tissue. Using it, she picked up one of the rectangles and folded it carefully into the tissue.

"Evidence," Sweets whispered, shoving the wad into her pocket.

The door opened suddenly, surprising them. Moogie stood before them in a fluorescent green and pink yoga outfit, spandex molding her perfect figure. Perfection ended at her face, which was marred by a sneer of distaste. Her long brown hair was twisted up in a knot on the top of her head. Her finely sculpted eyebrows narrowed.

"What are you doing here?"

"Hey, Moogie, we need to talk," Sweets said, pushing past her and entering the house. Shocked, Loretta slid by, nodding to Moogie as she passed.

Neither had been in Moogie's house before and they were surprised at the fine quality of the furnishings. Her living room looked like it had come out of a catalog. As Moogie shut the door after them, Loretta stood awkwardly against a wall while Sweets made herself comfortable on a white leather couch.

"What's this all about?" Moogie asked, glaring at Sweets.

"We heard you were boinking Bennie Uzul," Sweets said without preliminary.

"That's none of your business!"

"He's dead," Sweets said, scooting forward, keeping her eye on Moogie.

"I heard."

"Yeah, bad news carries fast. He was murdered, you know."

That startled her. "I . . . didn't know." Sweets noted her eyes blinking.

"So, you admit you knew him?"

"We dated a few times."

"Oh, come on, Moogie, you did more than that," Sweets pressed.

"So what? That's none of your business."

"Did you kill him?"

"Kill him? Of course not! You've got a lot of nerve. I want you to leave," Moogie demanded.

"I think you did," Sweets drawled, standing up and wandering around the room, picking up items. "In fact, I think you found out about him and all his other women. Then you killed him in a jealous rage."

Moogie laughed, highly pitched as if forced. "Don't be ridiculous. Me, jealous? Of what? The old bags who live here? No contest."

"So you knew there were other women?" Loretta asked.

Moogie turned to face her, surprised that she was in the room. "Of course. Bennie was a player. Don't I know you?"

"Yes. Loretta Dukes. We've met before. You objected to my Bible study," Loretta said, smiling awkwardly.

"That's right. I remember you now. Sorry about that. I just needed a bit of fun. This place was boring me to death."

"We're still meeting," Loretta said, "and you're always welcome, Moogie."

"That's because I gave it up. I met Bennie and you could say we got involved, but I'm sure you would call it divine intervention."

Loretta smiled. "I would."

Moogie smirked, rubbed her eyes and moved further away. Sweets resumed her seat on the white couch and Loretta sat next to her.

"Would you mind telling us about your . . . uh . . . relationship?" Loretta asked softly. "From what I've heard, he was quite a man."

"I'll say," Moogie whistled, throwing herself into an overstuffed chair. She hooked her leg over the armrest. "Whoo-wee, for an old guy, he was all man. I saw him at the pool, chatting up the women. Dumb broads. Couldn't see they were getting played."

"But you could," Sweets encouraged her.

"I'll say. He tried his sweet talk on me and I set him straight."

"I'm afraid I've been married so long that I haven't

a clue what that means. Did that make him interested in you?" Loretta asked, innocently.

Moogie stared at her and chuckled. "I don't want to shock you, Loretta, but I took him to bed that night."

Loretta did look shocked, which made Moogie laugh all the more. "After we had hot, raunchy sex, we used to lay in bed and make fun of the people here. They're so damn gullible really, especially the old women. They'd believe anything. And they call them the Great Generation! Ha ha."

Sweets narrowed her eyes and clenched her hand into a fist. Loretta placed hers over it. They exchanged looks and Sweets relaxed.

"So you knew he was taking advantage of them," Loretta said quietly.

"Well, of course! He loved to tell me about it. We would laugh and laugh."

"I can see how it'd be funny," Loretta smiled. "Ripe for the picking."

"You can say that again," Moogie laughed, slapping her thigh.

Sweets could stand it no longer. She stood up, her fists clenched at her side, her face red with fury. "And I suppose you told him who to go after. Did you tell him Maddie Ingersoll was wealthy and gullible? How about Madge Ziegler? Did you tell him she could be won over by appealing to her faith?"

Moogie's grin dissolved. Her eyes widened and she jumped to her feet.

"What of it? They deserved it. Silly old women thinking he was interested in them, and all along he was with me. It was too funny."

Loretta stood up, unsure of what to do. Sweets looked as if she was about to take a swing. She sent a prayer to heaven.

"And since you shared in this big joke, I supposed you also shared in the money he got out of them?" Sweets shouted. "And being the creep he was, he probably stiffed you. Is that why you killed him?" Sweets took a step closer. She shook off Loretta's warning hand. "Or did you get tired of his screwing around and kill him?"

Moogie took a step toward Sweets. "You're still not too smart, Sweets. I didn't kill him," she smiled wickedly, "and I wasn't jealous. I didn't care who he screwed, and it's not a crime when they give it willingly. Believe me, they were willing. Oh, so willing."

"You heartless bitch!" Sweets snarled, stepping even closer.

"Fat cow!"

"Slut!"

"Get out of my house before I throw you out!"

"Let's go, Sweets," Loretta said, stepping between the two women. She practically dragged Sweets to the door with Moogie following close behind.

"Yes, go! Get out of here and don't come back!"

"We're going," Sweets shouted back, "and you can kiss my ass."

"Who could miss it!" Moogie screamed, slamming the door.

"That was Loretta," Babe said, shutting the lid of her cell phone. "She and Sweets are on their way."

Cicie, Margarita, Boom Boom, Bella and Veronica paused their eating to listen. It was welcome news. They had been talking since they arrived at Just Yoking and hadn't made any progress. They were nearly finished with their breakfast.

"Wonder what they'll tell us. You think Moogie did it?" Cicie asked.

"Well, someone poisoned him," Veronica said in frustration.

"Poison is a woman's weapon," Cicie continued, "except Lady Macbeth who used a dagger."

"You're saying it's a woman, not a man," Veronica said between mouthfuls.

"It has to be Moogie," Boom Boom said, sipping on her orange juice.

"We'll have to wait until they get here," Bella responded.

"Let's hope Sweets didn't kill Moogie! Then

we'd have two murderers in our group." Boom Boom giggled.

"Josie did not kill Bennie!" Veronica said sharply.

"You're right, Veronica," Bella said, adding sugar to her coffee. "She doesn't have it in her. We all know that."

"I just can't believe we're going through this," Margarita pouted. "Have you heard from your daughter yet, Babe? This has to stop!"

"No," Babe said, pushing her plate away. "She'll call when she gets my message. She's very busy."

"Who else could have done it?" Cicie wondered out loud.

"Shall I read our list," Veronica asked, whipping out her smart phone. "Moogie's at the top, but we also have Gary Smith, John Fleming, Laura Breslin, Josie, Maddie, Boom Boom, Madge, Mimi, Rosie Davidson, Melanie Yaeger, and Cheryl Fortesque. Did I forget anyone?"

"Madame X," Cicie countered. "The unknown woman."

"I didn't kill him, so take me off the list, Veronica."

"You had the Merlot, Boom Boom," Cicie reminded her.

"But I didn't kill him! Anyone can get a bottle of Merlot at Wine and Such."

"Good point," Veronica said. "Let's buy a bottle to

show Detective Varland that anyone could get their hands on it. That should clear Boom Boom."

"I love the idea," Margarita said. "Let's go right now!"

"Let's wait for Sweets and Loretta."

"Laura shouldn't be on the list," Cicie argued. "She has no motive. And Cheryl Fortescue was gone before Bennie was killed."

"That's right," Boom Boom nodded, "and Maddie just doesn't have it in her."

"What about Mimi?" Veronica asked as she removed two names.

The ladies looked mournfully at each other. "Keep her," Cicie replied.

"What about Madge?"

"I can't see her doing it either," Margarita said.

"But you can see me?" Boom Boom huffed. "I like that. Great friends."

"Take Boom Boom off the list, Veronica," Bella instructed.

"That leaves Gary Smith, John Fleming, Josie, Mimi, Melanie and Rosie."

"And Moogie. Don't forget her!" Boom Boom added, pleased that she was no longer a suspect.

When the dishes were cleared and the waitress refilled their cups with fresh coffee, Sweets and Loretta arrived. The ladies scooted over and made room for them.

"It's her," Sweets announced. "It's Moogie. I've got the evidence."

"Don't jump to conclusions," Loretta cautioned. "She is definitely a suspect, but we don't know for sure."

"What evidence?" Boom Boom asked. "Tell us!"

Sweets looked around and then pulled a wadded tissue from her pocket. She unfolded it and the women bent forward to look at its contents. They saw a gray-green rectangle that looked like a dog treat.

"What is it?" Babe whispered.

"Rat poison. It was in front of Moogie's front door."

"Sweets, you've tampered with evidence!" Veronica exclaimed.

"Shh. I left the rest there. Detective Varland will want to see this. We're going to take it over to him and then he'll let Josie go."

"So, Moogie killed him," Margarita whispered. "Why?"

"They were partners," Sweets hissed, "and Bennie stiffed her."

"No time to lose. Let's go see Chief Varland!" Boom Boom insisted.

The ladies swiftly settled their individual bills, grabbed their doggie bags and piled into Bella's and Loretta's cars, Sweets following on her motorcycle.

CHAPTER NINETEEN

When she left her house at five that morning, Vana Aguda had no idea how crazy her day would become. As secretary to the Homicide Division, she expected a certain amount of chaos, but nothing like what was to come.

She was an attractive woman in her forties, with flawless dark skin and almond shaped eyes. Her shiny black hair was kept under control by a complicated system of braiding that included beads. She was proud of her hourglass figure, which she dressed to accentuate. That morning she dressed in a red silk dress that was cinched at the waist with a wide belt. She wore red flats on her feet. She always wore flats because she was constantly on the move taking care of her detectives.

They were like her family. Joey Rinaldi was her darling boy and he knew it. She made sure he didn't get too full of himself by pointing out his faults, lovingly, of course. Norm Luskowitz was her big teddy bear, but he could scare paint off a wall. He was always bringing her flowers from his garden. In return, she made sure he had a ready supply of Baby Ruths and Snickers in his desk drawer. Mateo Garza was her awkward boy, a real nerd. He was terrified about becoming a daddy and since she had two of her own, he eagerly accepted her advice on how to be a parent. She made sure he got away from his computer before he went blind.

She had a special fondness for the Chief. She worried constantly about him. Magnus was working himself into an early grave. She did her best to slow down the inevitable erosion, but he was a stubborn man. He didn't take care of himself, so she vowed to take care of him herself. The other detectives had wives, but Magnus was alone. She couldn't understand it. He was a good-looking man, strong, dependable, a real catch but didn't have a clue on how to find a good woman. She couldn't remember the last time he was on a date. What was he waiting for?

She made sure he ate breakfast, always bringing him an egg sandwich and orange juice in the morning. Even though it wasn't in her job description, she picked up his dry cleaning and made sure he had a fresh shirt and a selection of ties hidden in a file drawer. He had a tendency to spill coffee on himself.

She was responsible for the entire Peralta Canyon Homicide Division. Besides answering phones and escorting visitors, she responded to emails, made copies, kept the detectives' expense accounts, managed Varland's calendar, and prepared the final reports for Commander Hayes.

When she came into the precinct that morning, she hit the ground running. The Benito Uzul murder investigation was generating a lot of paperwork. She had spent the morning cataloging the contents of his file bin.

She looked over at Magnus and Mateo; their heads were together in front of the victim's laptop. They were still going over the emails. She looked at her watch. It was almost noon. She would have to interfere. They needed to get some lunch and rest their eyes.

Her intercom buzzed. It was Greg, the desk sergeant, asking for her help. She was nearly finished with her task, so she wasn't happy to have to stop just to help him out. She made her way down the hallway and into the lobby.

"What is it, Sergeant? I've got a lot of work to do."

"Sorry, Vana, but I didn't want to call Detective Varland as they requested. They say they have evidence in the Benito Uzul murder case. I don't know what to do with them."

"Who?" she asked.

He pointed behind her. Squished together on the bench against the wall were six elderly women, waiting expectantly, with their purses in their laps. Their heads perked up as she approached.

"Excuse me, we need to see Chief Varland," one old dear said, as she rose to her feet and came towards her. She was tiny, about eighty or so, wearing white capris pants and a striped blouse. She clutched a white leather purse against her body. "Can you take us to him, please?"

"We've got evidence in a murder case!" boomed a tall, imposing woman with short white hair. She was dressed in white slacks and a sparkly purple blouse, with a white blazer. Vana noticed prominent sapphires in her ear lobes and an impressive sapphire necklace.

"We know who killed Bennie Uzul," said a third woman with cropped white hair. She looked like a biker's grandmother.

"Now, Sweets, we don't know that for sure," countered a slender, attractive woman wearing red capris and a white tunic, touching her friend's arm. "You don't want to make wild accusations in a police station."

"They're not wild," Sweets answered. "They're cold, hard facts!"

"Go on. Show her," said a petite, white-haired woman, hobbling forward on crippled feet.

"I'm not showing it to her, Babe," Sweets argued. "It's for Detective Varland's eyes only."

"Can you take us to him, please?" the tall woman with sapphires asked.

"He's got to see us!" said a woman with dark hair who stepped in front of the rest. She had an exotic cast to her face.

"It's urgent!" cried a younger woman with long

blond hair, who pushed past the dark haired woman. "We must see him right now!"

Vana didn't know what to do as they quickly surrounded her. She was suddenly mute as the women began talking between themselves, the decibel level gradually climbing as they argued about what they wanted her to do.

"Shut up!" she shouted, surprising herself. They fell silent, but their eyes spoke volumes. "Excuse me for shouting. I'm sorry, ladies, but Detective Varland has gone to lunch. You'll have to come back later."

"Then we'll wait," said the sweet little dumpling with the bad feet.

The women agreed and followed her back to the bench where they sat.

At that moment, Detective Varland rushed into the lobby, his suit coat flung over his shoulder.

"There you are. I'm going to lunch, Vana. Can you help Mateo? The printer's jammed again."

"Yes, sir," Vana said, maneuvering herself between him and the ladies who had jumped up to waylay him. "I'll take care of it. Have a nice lunch."

"Hello, Chief! We've got some evidence for you."

He stopped and was quickly surrounded. "Boom Boom! Ladies! What are you doing here?"

"Josie didn't do it and we can prove it!" Sweets yelled.

"We know who did it, Detective Varland," Boom Boom announced.

They all started talking at once until he put his hand up.

"Vana, will you take these ladies to the conference room, get them some coffee, and then help Mateo with the printer. I need those emails printed out."

Vana was defeated. It was just like Magnus to skip lunch to help out a bunch of senior citizens. It made her mad, but she was so used to obeying him, that she quickly showed the women to the conference room. They were extremely pleased with themselves and started clucking like a bunch of chickens as soon as they seated themselves.

She went to the break room and found that the remaining coffee was like sludge. She quickly cleaned the pot and brewed some fresh. After that, she went to help Mateo with the printer.

Detective Varland entered the conference room with his suit coat on and his tie straightened. He sat at the head of the table.

"Now, what's all this about evidence? You know, tampering with evidence is a crime. I hope I'm not going to have to arrest you."

"You've already arrested two of our group, isn't that enough for you?" Margarita stormed.

"Don't jump down his throat. He's only doing his job." Loretta tried to soothe her.

"We didn't tamper with evidence, Detective, but we did collect some," Sweets admitted.

"Show him," Babe demanded. "I want to get out of here."

"Show him, Sweets," Bella encouraged.

Sweets pulled out the wad of tissue from her pocket. She pushed it toward the detective. Varland got up and pulled the tissue towards him. He unwrapped it and stared.

"What is it?" he asked, completely perplexed.

"Rat poison!" Sweets stated triumphantly. "I recognized it immediately."

"Where did you get it?"

"You tell him, Loretta," Sweets prompted.

"At Moogie's house. She has a whole bunch in front of her doorway. We only took one so we could show you."

"We think she killed him," Boom Boom whispered *soto voce*.

"Moogie?" the detective's eyes narrowed and he took a second look at the gray-green rectangle in the tissue. "You know Moogie? What's her real name?"

"Margaret Googin. She's in Unit #1000. She's an accomplice of Bennie Uzul. She admitted as much to us," Loretta declared. "Isn't that right, Sweets?"

"It sure is, Detective Varland. She put Bennie onto

the women with money who would be easy marks," Sweets added. "Like Maddie Ingersoll. She laughed about it. Told us she and Bennie used to make fun of us old, dumb broads."

"When we confronted her, she just laughed and said it wasn't a crime if they gave their money willingly," Loretta continued. "I don't know if that's true, but I do know it's wrong. I admit that if I weren't a Christian woman I might have decked her."

"Loretta! I can't believe what I'm hearing," Veronica exclaimed. "You almost hit her?"

"No, but I wanted to and I'm very sorry about it. It's a terrible witness."

"I would have, but Loretta got between us," Sweets boasted.

"That's very interesting," Varland said. "She actually admitted that she was part of his con game?"

The ladies all nodded.

"Did she admit to killing him?"

"No-o," Sweets admitted, "but she has motive. He was probably stiffing her. It'd be just like him, don't you think? Con conning a con. She has a terrible temper, Detective. She's perfectly capable of it. And she hates us because we use the pool, which she thinks she owns. She probably set Josie up to take the fall!"

"I see," he said. "Did you give her a bottle of your Merlot, Boom Boom?"

"Wha-at? No! Not her. I wouldn't let her even enter my house, let alone give her one of my best bottles of . . . oh."

"But she could have bought it at Wine and Such, just like Boom Boom," Bella argued. "Show him, Veronica."

Veronica stood and pulled a bottle of Merlot from her large purse and set it on the table. "It's the same brand as Boom Boom's," she said. "Anyone could buy it, even Moogie; so, you see, she could have done it."

"Please let Josie go," Bella implored.

"Yes, let her go! Let her go! She's innocent!" The women's shrill voices overlapped until Varland felt like he was drowning in a whirlpool. He held up his hand and they went silent, looking up at him with eyes full of hope. He hated to disappoint them.

"I'll look into it. Thank you for bringing this to my attention. I'll have it analyzed."

"We knew we could count on you, Chief!" Boom Boom said, standing to her feet.

"Can we wait here while you go get Josie?" Babe asked.

"Hmm. No. Sorry. I'm afraid I'll have to keep her a little longer. Why don't you all go home? I promise I'll check this out."

At that moment, Vana entered with cups and a pot of coffee. She could see Magnus was sweating and unsure of how to get out of the situation. She could also see that the ladies were less than pleased with what he had just told them. It was time for her to take action.

"Detective Varland, you're wanted in the squad room. It's urgent."

He quickly took the out she gave him. "Excuse me, ladies. I'm afraid I must leave. Vana will show you out. I'll be in touch. Have no fear."

He practically ran out of the room.

Vana gave them each a cup, filled it with coffee and waited while they sipped on the foul beverage. It wasn't long before she was able to escort them out of the building.

CHAPTER TWENTY

The woman who opened the door surprised him. She was about his age, maybe younger, with long, curly brunette hair, and was dressed to kill. She wore a tight fitting halter-top, knee-length dress made of some kind of shimmery silver material that hugged her body and silver, open-toed spiked heels. At first glance, she was gorgeous, but on second glance he saw a hardened face with cold brown eyes. Her naked face was a sharp contrast to her clothed body.

"Why, hello there. How can I help you?" she said in a low husky voice.

"Detective Magnus Varland, Homicide Division, PCPD," he replied, showing his badge. He watched her demeanor transform as she pulled the door closed ever so slightly and peered through the opening.

"What do you want?"

"Just a few questions. Won't take a minute. May I come in?"

"Oh, all right," she scowled. She threw the door open and walked back into the house, leaving Varland to follow after her. He could hear her heels *click, click, clicking* on the tile floor and found her in the kitchen, eating from a cup of yogurt.

"Make it quick. I've got a date and haven't put my face on yet."

"Sure thing, Ms. Googin. Mind if we sit in the living room?"

"Suit yourself. What's this all about anyway?"

"It's about Bennie Uzul," he said, finding an over-stuffed chair to sit in. He watched her arrange herself on a white leather couch, crossing her long, muscular legs to good effect.

"What about him? Heard he was murdered."

"You are well-informed. I understand you knew him."

"Sure, guy got around. He liked the ladies, and as you can see for yourself, I'm not bad to look at. I knew him."

"How well?"

"Just a few laughs now and then. Nothing serious."

"Really? According to my information, you and he were more than friends. In fact, the two of you spent quite a bit of time in Vegas together."

"Yeah, we went to Vegas. So what?"

"The two of you corresponded quite frequently by email, didn't you?"

That got her attention. "Who doesn't nowadays?"

"I have Bennie's laptop, Ms. Googin. I've read your emails."

"Hey, what is this? Did those two bitches put you on to me?"

"What two bitches?"

"Yeah, you know who I mean. Jocelyn Sweets and

Loretta Dukes. I knew I shouldn't have let them in this morning. Couple of busybodies. What'd they do, go right down to the station after I kicked them out and tell you I was in league with Bennie? Fleecing the pigeons in this place? That I killed him in a jealous rage? It's all bullshit!"

"That's why I'm here," Varland assured her. "I want to get your side of the story."

"Damn right. Sure I knew about him dipping his toe in other waters, but it meant nothing to me. He was my guy and as you can see, there's no contest between me and the old broads in this place. I wasn't worried. I sure as hell didn't kill him in a jealous rage! The idea is laughable."

"I'm glad you cleared that up for me, Ms. Googin."

"Yeah, well, just because me and Sweets have history, doesn't give her the right to accuse me. She never forgave me for hitting her in the eye."

"You were in a fight with her?"

"Nah, nothing like that. I like to swim laps and she and the other old bags take up the whole pool with their damn exercising. I tried to stay close to the side, but Sweets just kept moving into my lane. I accidentally hit her in the eye when I passed by. She said I did it on purpose. She's never forgotten it."

"Are you talking about the Superstition Aquatics Club?"

"That's what they call themselves. They just

bounce around in the water. That's not exercising. I swim 250 laps a day. That's why I look the way I do."

"I can see you're very . . . fit, Ms. Googin."

"Call me Moogie. Everyone does." She leaned forward pressing her arms against her chest to emphasize the curve of her breasts under the shimmering fabric. She leaned back and sensually crossed her legs the other direction. "Me and Bennie, it was just for laughs. We didn't take each other seriously. He had plans and so did I. I'm a widow, you know."

"I didn't. I'm sorry for your loss."

"Don't be. The guy was over ninety. His time had come. I gave him two good years anyway. But, I'm still young and I like to fool around as long as I have my looks. I work out every day. Want to feel my bicep?"

"No, that's okay."

"Come on. I won't bite."

"Do you like wine, Ms. Googin?"

"Wine? Yuk. I don't drink alcohol, Detective. Too many calories. I have to watch my figure," she replied, rubbing her hands along her thighs.

"Were you in on the scheme to bilk Maddie Ingersoll out of $20,000?"

That got her attention. "What? No way!"

"Are you sure about that? According to your emails, you did. I've got one here that should interest you."

He reached into his suit jacket and pulled out a folded piece of paper. He handed it over to her. As she read it he could see the color in her face heighten and then drain away.

"So I told him the old bag was rich and a bit senile. So what."

"You were in on his plan to bilk her out of her money. That's aiding and abetting in grand larceny, Ms. Googin."

"I have to get ready for my date," she said, alarmed, standing up. The harshness in her face returned and she was no longer attractive. Her eyebrows narrowed and her mouth twisted into a snarl. "I've answered enough questions."

"Did you find out he was leaving the state? Was he leaving before he gave you your cut? Did that make you angry?"

"I said I'm done answering questions!"

"It's here or at the station, Ms. Googin. Your date will have to wait."

She sat back down and crossed her arms, scowling. "I didn't kill him."

"Where were you between four and six Wednesday morning? Think hard."

"I was out."

"Can anyone corroborate that?"

"Yeah. Reggie Hightower."

"Could you give me Mr. Hightower's address?"

"I'd rather not. He's married."

"He's your alibi. I'm sure you'll want me to check."

She stood up and went to her purse on a counter in front of the window. She pulled out a white business card and handed it to him.

"You can call him at his office. He'll tell you I was with him."

"He's not your date this evening?"

"No."

"May I ask who you're seeing?"

"If you must know, I'm seeing Gary Smith."

"The maintenance man here at the resort?"

"Yeah, what of it? He's not a bad looking guy."

"I don't think I have to tell you not to leave town, Ms. Googin. I may have a few more questions for you and possibly Mr. Smith."

"You can talk to me through my attorney next time, Detective."

"Fair enough. Thank you for your time. Oh, by the way, is that rat poison I saw in front of your door?"

CHAPTER TWENTY-ONE

The air conditioner wasn't working when Detective Varland entered the homicide room around two o'clock. It was over 100 degrees indoors. He took off his coat, pulled a handkerchief from his back pocket, and wiped his brow and neck. He stopped at Detective Rinaldi's desk and rapped his knuckles on the marred wood.

"Whew-ee, it's hotter than Hades in here. Is that thing on the blink again?"

"Waits for the hottest day of the year to die. Maintenance says they'll have it going in an hour or so." Rinaldi wiped his forehead, and then smoothed back a strand of limp black hair. His suit coat was off and his sleeves were rolled up to his elbows. Beads of sweat glistened on his upper lip. He wiped it with the back of his hand.

"What'd the Commander say?"

"He's on board. We'll pursue the Googin lead if this doesn't pan out. If nothing else, we've got her on aiding and abetting. Did you exercise the search warrant on the Simone house?"

"Rat poison in her storage unit. Husband said he was trying to get rid of mice. They should have gotten a cat. More natural. Part of the food chain, you know.

They had a stack of those plastic cups, too. Bagged those. We arrested her on suspicion of murder."

"Good. Croquet mallet?"

"We're still looking. She probably disposed of it."

"Once Clement matches her DNA to the sample from the victim's t-shirt, we'll charge her with murder. Good job, Rinaldi."

"Thanks, Chief. Sheesh, I almost forgot! There's a federal agent sitting in your office."

"A fed? What for?"

"Search me. She's been in there about ten minutes."

"She?"

"M-hm. Good looking woman, too. Be nice. She might be the one."

Varland rubbed his jaw and felt the bristles on his face. He put his suit coat back on and straightened his tie. He rubbed his hands through his sandy hair, knowing he was only making it worse. He opened the door.

She was standing at the window, peeking through the blinds at the street outside. She had smooth blond hair curling under at the neck, a trim figure covered in a white blouse tucked into slim black slacks and a confident stance that only comes from military training. He was alarmed to find his blood pumping a little bit harder. Rushing wind filled his ears as she turned around.

Her mouth, smiling easily, revealed even white

teeth, whiter than anything he had ever seen. Next were her eyes, small blue orbs that glittered like starlight. She extended her hand. No fingernail polish, just gleaming buffed nails. He shook it and appreciated her firm handshake.

"Special Agent Petey Winters, CIA. Before you say anything, I want to assure you that I am not here to cause you trouble."

"How reassuring. Would you care to sit down and tell me how I can help? You do want my help, don't you? That why you're here?"

She sat, folding her slender legs, ankles crossed, under the chair. She turned her palms upwards and gave him a radiant smile.

"It's my mother, you see," she said, surprising him. "What kind of a daughter would I be if I didn't come and help her?"

"I'm not following," he responded, feeling his lips turn upward.

"My mother is Babe Winters, leader of the Superstition Aquatics Club. Ever hear of it?"

He groaned involuntarily and she laughed. He chuckled as well.

"Lovely bunch of ladies," he smiled. "They've been hindering my investigation, tampering with evidence and messing with my witnesses. But, I can't help but love them."

She laughed an easy, infectious laugh. He smiled broadly.

"She called me begging for my help. I took the first plane out from DC. I don't know what she thinks I can do, but she's very concerned about her friend, Mimi Bradshaw."

"Ah, Mimi," he said, sitting more straight in his chair. "She is no longer a suspect."

"That's good. Mother will be so relieved."

"We've arrested Josie Simone."

"Good for you."

"She's also in your mother's club."

"Oh." She frowned. "Bad for me. Mother will never understand. I'm sure you have your reasons?" She looked up at him. His heart nearly stopped. Her blue eyes, framed by long curling lashes, were like two cool pools. He wanted to dive into them. He wanted her to smile again.

"I'll be happy to share what we have with you, Agent Winters."

She smiled and the room lit up like a light had flicked on. Before he went over the bend, he realized Vana had entered the room and flicked on the overhead light, which she often did. It drove her crazy that he worked in the dark.

"Mrs. Simone's lawyer is here, sir."

"Is there anything I can do to help, Detective Varland?" Agent Winters asked. "I'm here unofficially, to reassure Mother, but if you can use my help . . ." She left the invitation hanging in the air.

"Well, if you want to see our murder room, I have no objections. I'll be back in a minute. It's this way."

He led her to the small alcove that served as their murder room. He was conscious of how tattered and unsubstantial it appeared. She didn't seem to notice and went to the board where the murder photos were thumbtacked, along with written post-it notes on the case.

"Anything else you need, Special Agent Winters?"

"I'd like to see the body, if possible." She turned from the photo of Bennie Uzul lying on the poolside concrete. She grinned, but her eyes were cold.

"It's at the medical examiner's in Phoenix. May I ask why?"

She smiled again, but the warmth wasn't there. "Curiosity?"

He smiled back. "I'll be happy to drive you, Agent Winters."

"No need. I've got a car," she replied.

He gave her his most winning smile and raised his hands palms up. "Please. I need to get out of this hothouse. My car has great air conditioning. Besides, I know the way."

She smiled her easy smile, teeth and all, and nodded.

He drove while she perused the case file. His car's air conditioner wafted a faint smell of her perfume to his nose. It was nice. He tried to place it, but couldn't. He glanced at her, but she appeared absorbed in the material.

He was pleased with himself. It was a pretty solid case. He had Josie Simone's fingerprints on one of the washers in the Laundromat. They found rat poison at her house, along with the same plastic cups used to administer the poison-laced wine, and a witness who could confirm that she had access to her bottles of Merlot, the same Merlot that had contained the strychnine. She had admitted that she had been with the victim within the time frame of the murder. She had also confessed that he was leaving her. A woman scorned was a good motive for murder. She had means, opportunity, and motive.

As far as Margaret Googin was concerned, the rat poison the ladies had supplied did not contain strychnine, but bromethalin. Reggie Hightower had reluctantly admitted he was with her during the time of the murder. She was not his murderer, but he had issued a warrant to have her arrested for aiding and abetting in grand larceny.

They walked into the Forensics Lab together. He escorted her to the observation room. He could see Clement finishing an autopsy on a young black male.

"Ugh. I can never get used to it?" she said in disgust.

"Autopsies?"

"Death," she stated flatly.

They watched as Clement made the last stitch on the body. An attendant hovered nearby and when he was finished wheeled the body out of the room. Varland rapped on the window. Clement looked up, smiled and waved for him to come into the room.

As they entered, the smell was almost more than Varland could stand and he looked quickly at Agent Winters who appeared not to notice.

"Hey, Magnus, didn't expect you again today. Who's this pretty lady?" Clement inquired, giving Varland's companion an appreciative glance. He pulled off his latex gloves and apron and disposed of them in a hazardous waste bin.

Before he could introduce her, Agent Winters stuck out her hand and firmly shook Clement's. "Special Agent Petey Winters, Dr. Clement. Detective Varland said I might take a look at Benito Uzul's body."

Covering his surprise, Clement turned and beckoned them to follow without a word. He led them to the refrigeration unit. He opened a drawer and pulled out a sliding pallet, revealing the corpse. Agent Winters moved in closer and stared at the body.

"No one's claimed him yet?" Clement asked,

looking at Varland with a mixture of professional inquiry and personal amusement.

"No. No living relatives as far as we know."

"We'll keep it for about a month and then cremate."

"That's fine. We have all we need, I believe," Varland replied, keeping an eye on the woman, who appeared to be scrutinizing the torso with her piercing blue eyes. "We've made an arrest."

"Excellent. I should have the DNA results tomorrow. That'll seal the deal. Are you looking for something, Agent Winters?" Clement asked, moving in beside her.

She flinched at his nearness but recovered quickly. "Did you find any tattoos on the body, Dr. Clement?"

"Several. See here on his neck he has three stars and there's a scorpion on his back right shoulder. Here." He lifted the body and she peered at it. She shook her head and Clement lowered the shoulder. He suddenly brightened. "He had a blooded dagger on his left ankle. Want to see that?"

"No. Is that all?"

"I believe so. Are you looking for something specific?"

"Numbers."

"Numbers, hmm. I don't think I found any numbers," Clement said, giving the corpse a once over. He began lifting the arms and legs of the corpse and examining them.

She looked deeply disappointed. "Thank you for your time."

"Is there something you want to tell me," Varland drawled, feeling a little miffed that she had bamboozled him.

"Hold on, Agent Winters," Clement exclaimed. "Here! Between his fingers. They're very small. There's a three, an eight and I believe this is a two. Let's check the other hand. Right. Here's a six, or it could be a nine, another three and a one. Well, I'll be. Can't figure how I missed them."

"Do you know what they mean?" Varland asked, fixing his eyes on her with an interrogative stare.

She met his gaze with a look of puzzlement and indecision. She broke away and shook her head.

"It's an old cipher from the Cold War," she said with a catch in her voice.

Varland was at a loss. He was completely baffled. "Cold War? What's that got to do with my murder victim?"

"It's freezing in here. Do you think we could talk somewhere else?"

"Sure thing," Clement reassured her. He pushed the pallet back into the drawer and shut the door. "This way," he said, taking her arm and leading her out of the room. Varland followed in a state of shock.

"You haven't been straight with me, Special Agent Winters," Varland said gruffly. "You told me you were here unofficially. What does the CIA have to do with this?"

They were sitting across from one another in the pristine break room. Clement bustled about at the counter, fixing cups of coffee, glancing over his shoulder at his friend who was about to lose his temper.

She appeared to slump in her chair, pressed down by an unseen force. Her bowed face was covered by the fall of her blond hair.

"I am," she said quietly.

"What?" Varland demanded, grinding his teeth.

"Here unofficially."

"I don't believe you."

She looked up and he was struck by the grief that cast a shadow on her face. She appeared to be wrestling with what to say and what not to say.

"I don't blame you. I wasn't completely honest with you. It's funny how things come together, don't you think?"

"I don't understand," he said, pulling back from his anger and adjusting to his desire to console her. "What has come together?"

Clement chose that moment to set steaming cups of coffee and a plate of his wife's cookies in front of them. He sat at the end of the table and shifted his eyes from his friend to the woman. He could feel the tension between them. Inside, he was gleeful. He hadn't seen his friend so flummoxed by a woman in a long time. There was hope for him yet.

"I picked up your police inquiry into Benito Ordaz. His name was red-flagged. At the same time, my mother called asking me to help her friend who was charged with the murder of Bennie Uzul, aka Benito Ordaz. Is it a coincidence, you think? Or divine providence?"

"I'm not following," Varland murmured, picking up his cup and sipping on the hot liquid. It burned his lips and he spilled some on his tie. He glanced at Clement and could see the old man's eyes glittering with suppressed interest.

Appearing to have made a decision, Agent Winter squared her shoulders, straightened in her chair and looked him in the eyes.

"I can tell you because most of this has been declassified. His real name is Borysko Orlyk. He was born in the Ukraine and immigrated to Venezuela in the forties. His parents changed their names and immigrated to the United States soon after. They settled in California."

"I thought he was born in Venezuela," Varland growled. "What else don't I know?"

"He was recruited by the Company in '73 because of his Ukrainian background and his fluency in the language."

"That's when he went off the grid," Varland

responded. "We wondered about that. He was arrested but never served any time."

"Yes. He was made for the job; he was smart, ruthless, and fluent in the Ukrainian dialect. He also was highly motivated because he didn't want to go to jail.

"He was trained to infiltrate the National Labor Alliance in the Ukraine to undermine Soviet control. He spent ten years there before he returned to the States and resigned from the CIA. He subsequently disappeared. It took a few years, but eventually it was discovered that during his time in the Ukraine, he had become a double agent. He had been feeding us misinformation while providing the Soviets with information on our operations."

"So the government is interested?"

She blushed crimson and tried to regain control by snatching the coffee and gulping the hot beverage. She cried out and began coughing.

Clement jumped up and patted her on the back while passing her a napkin to blot up the spilled liquid on the table. She smiled her appreciation and he returned to his seat.

She cleared her throat. "Forgive me. This is very hard for me. No, the government isn't involved. I didn't tell them about your inquiry into Benito Ordaz. As I said, coincidentally Mother called me yesterday about her friend and gave me an excuse to come out here and see for myself."

"Again, I'm not following you, Agent Winters," Varland confessed. He was back to wanting her to smile. He hated seeing her struggle with her tightly held emotions.

"Call me Petey. After all, I am unofficially here," she demurred, giving him a weak smile.

"That's an unusual name. Where's it come from?" Clement piped in. He felt the need to give her some breathing room. Varland scowled at him.

She turned her gaze on Clement and smiled, showing her pretty white teeth. "It's a nickname. Don't tell anyone, but my name is Petronilla."

"Good god!" Clement exhaled. "What were your parents thinking?"

She laughed at that and the tension eased.

"I was named after a great aunt who helped my mother's family get out of Germany during the war. In basic training, they shortened it to Petey and it stuck. Just one of the boys, you know."

"You were saying," Varland pressed, giving Clement the evil eye.

She turned her blue orbs on him and he felt his senses blur.

"In 1978, two CIA operatives, John Priestly and Michael Coughlin, were killed in East Germany during a bogus defection. After Borysko Orlyk returned to the States and disappeared, they uncovered his role in their deaths. He had leaked their names to the East

Germans. He has been on the CIA's most wanted list ever since."

"A goddamn traitor!" Clement swore. "And to think I stitched him up so nicely!"

"Yes, he was a murderer and a traitor," she nodded, her eyes flashing.

"Living all these years in Arizona," Varland murmured, wiping his forehead. "Right here in my precinct."

"There's something else you should know," Petey continued, her eyes filling with tears. "John Priestly was my father."

"I thought you said your name is Winters."

"I took my stepfather's name when my mother remarried. I don't expect you to understand, but when his alias was red-flagged, I had to come. I had to see for myself. I had to see his body to know that he was really dead."

Silence filled the room. All three sat without looking at each other, absorbed in their own thoughts.

"What about the numbers?" Clement asked, breaking the silence.

"They're for identification." She pulled out a slip of paper from her pocket. She pushed it over to Varland.

He picked it up and read it out loud. "Six, three, one, three, eight, two."

"The i.d. for Borysko Orlyk. It's him. He's finally dead. Murdered. I can't say I'm sorry. He deserved worse, but justice is finally served. My father and Michael Coughlin have been avenged. May they rest in peace."

"It's still murder," Varland said softly, handing the paper back to her. "After she's arraigned, you can thank Josie Simone yourself."

"I will," she said. "If you don't mind taking me back to my car, I need to be with Mother. I'm not sure if I'll tell her or not, but she needs me. We're going to do everything we can to see that Josie has the best defense possible. She has done us a great service."

"If you ask me, she should get a medal," Clement enjoined, frowning at Varland.

CHAPTER TWENTY-TWO

He dropped Petey Winters off at her car. He watched her drive away and felt a yearning that he hadn't felt for many years. He had to admit she had gotten under his skin. He didn't for a minute believe she had told him everything, but he admired her. She was a cipher and he longed to decode her.

"Hey, Chief," Detective Garza welcomed him. "Congratulations on the arrest."

Varland smiled and stopped at his desk. "Congratulations, yourself. Your research paid off. You'll never believe it, but that Uzul character was really a Cold War double agent, a traitor and a murderer."

"A spy! Well, how do you like that! Wait'll Sofia hears. I can tell her, can't I? It's not a state secret, is it?"

"I don't think so. I think Petey would have told me if it were."

"Petey?"

"That's right. You weren't here when she came in. Petey Winters, Special Agent with the CIA. She caught your inquiry and flew in from DC to confirm his identity."

"I love it when a case falls together so neatly as this, eh, Chief?"

"Knock on wood," Varland said, rapping the desk with his knuckles.

"We've decided on a name, sir."

"You have?"

"Rosa, if it's a girl and Magnus if it's a boy," Garza beamed at Varland.

"I'm touched, Mateo, but you don't want to saddle the kid with a name like mine. It's too old-fashioned. How about Mateo Junior?"

"Well, what'd ya know. Mateo Junior. Why didn't I think of that?"

Having solved Mateo's baby dilemma, Varland was in a good mood when he went into his office, but it didn't last long. He sat down in his chair, propped his feet on the desk, leaned back with his arms behind his head, and thought about a certain woman with nice legs and an indescribable smile. Vana entered the room, flicked on the overhead light and ruined everything.

"There's someone to see you, Chief," she said.

"Let 'em wait. I don't want anything to spoil my good mood."

"'Fraid I can't. She's been waiting an hour. I'll bring her back, shall I?"

"Not another one of those Superstition women!"

"I don't know, sir. Well, what do you want me to do?"

"Oh, alright. Bring her back."

Vana left and he dropped his feet onto the floor.

Of all the confounded interruptions! But then again, maybe it was Petey's mother, Babe Winters. He jumped up and put his suit coat on. He drew his fingers through his hair and waited.

He immediately recognized Madge Ziegler as Vana let her in. He had interviewed her the day of the murder, just before he had gone to see Maddie Ingersoll. He stood as she entered. She was almost as tall as he. She would have been six feet tall, but for her hunched shoulders due, no doubt, from a bad back. She was wearing a white cotton pullover with blue flowers embroidered around the neck and white cotton pants. She looked like a Sunday school teacher. He rushed over to help her into the chair and received a pained expression for his efforts. He quickly sat back in his chair and gave her his most benevolent and patient smile.

"What can I do for you, Mrs. Ziegler?"

"It's Miss. I've come to confess."

He was startled. "Confess to what?"

"Why, to the murder of Bennie Uzul. I killed him."

"You don't say, and how did you kill him?"

"With a . . . croquet mallet."

He was shocked and his eyes widened. How did she know about the croquet mallet? She must have heard it from that Fleming woman. He knew she was a blabbermouth. But, fortunately for Miss Ziegler, she didn't know anything about the rat poison.

"Oh, and I poisoned him, too," Madge said, nodding.

Her admission took the wind out of his theory. Had he arrested the wrong woman?

"What kind of poison, ma'am?"

"Rat poison! I killed him with rat poison and pushed him into the pool. Josie had nothing to do with it. I killed him."

"Let me get this straight, you're confessing to the murder of Bennie Uzul?"

"That's what I said, didn't I? Josie had nothing to do with it."

"Why don't you tell me all about it. Start from the beginning."

"The beginning of what?"

"Well, how you did it."

"Oh, right. It's like this. I heard about him and Josie and went to see for myself. I was waiting outside the Laundromat until they were . . . finished and then I crept in and bashed him over the head with the croquet mallet."

"And the poison?"

"Oh! The poison. Right. Well, when he was out cold on the floor I poured a cup of wine laced with rat poison down his throat."

"Then you pushed him into the pool. How'd you do that?"

"What? How'd I do what?"

"Get him into the pool," Varland said patiently.

"I pulled him out of the Laundromat and pushed him into the pool."

"Why?"

"Because I didn't want someone to come in to do laundry and see him lying on the floor, that's why. What a fool question."

"How's your back, Miss Ziegler?"

"My back's fine. What's that got to do with tea in China?"

"Don't you have chronic back problems?"

"Well, I would have, wouldn't I? I had to drag him to the pool. He didn't weigh that much, but I'm sure you're aware, Detective, that dead weight takes more effort to move. I hurt my back pulling him to the pool. I've been going to my chiropractor for days now. I'm a lot stronger than I look, Detective."

"Why did you kill him, Miss Ziegler?"

"Please call me Madge. No one calls me Miss Ziegler except for the children I used to teach at Walker Elementary."

"Why did you kill him, Madge?"

"Because he was going to defraud my church and I didn't want Reverend Julian to be humiliated in front of his congregation. I've been going to that church for nearly twenty years, ever since I moved to Superstition Way Resort, and it's like my second home. He was an evil man, Detective. He led me on. I thought he was sincere in his faith, but he was just a wolf in sheep's clothing. Why, I even gave him some of my own money! I'm on a fixed income and it came dear, but I thought I was helping a truth-seeker, but he was just a con man."

She pulled a tissue from her pant's pocket and dabbed at her eyes. Varland wanted to resurrect Bennie Uzul just so he could strangle him to death. He waited while Madge composed herself.

"Aren't you going to arrest me?"

"Not right now. Tell me more about his scheme to defraud your church. What is the name of it?"

"Path of Light Tabernacle on Idaho Street."

"And Reverend Julian, what is his full name?"

"Why do you want to know that? I tell you, I killed Bennie Uzul."

"Just getting the facts, ma'am. Nothing sinister about it."

"I'm sorry, Detective. My faith in humanity has been sorely tested. It's Reverend James Julian. He came to our church as a new minister about ten years ago. He and his lovely wife, Beth, have a beautiful family, two boys and two girls; Matthew is eight, Luke is six, Leah is five and baby Joanna is nine months. She was a Christmas surprise. I've been there as each one was born."

Varland observed her as she sat serenely in her chair reflecting, no doubt, on the family she had adopted as her own. He could see she would be very protective of them and proceeded carefully.

"And Bennie tried to defraud them. I can see why you killed him. Tell me more."

She looked startled by his statement, but she swallowed with some difficulty and continued her narrative. "You can't imagine how guilty I feel for bringing Bennie into the church. Truly, Detective, I thought his conversion was genuine. I introduced him to Reverend Julian. They became friends almost immediately. I think they had him over for dinner a few times. Can you imagine it; eating at someone's table knowing you were lying to them the whole time. It is too horrible to imagine."

"Go on, Madge. What happened between Mr. Uzul and the good Reverend?"

"Next thing I knew, the Elder Board met to nominate Bennie to become an elder. He had only just become a Christian, so I was surprised, but I trusted them to know God's will. Word leaked out that Bennie had promised to donate $150,000! Everyone was so grateful. It was enough money to pay off our building debt and begin construction on our school. Everyone was talking about it. Bennie was the most popular guy at our church."

"When did you learn the truth, Madge?"

"Not for awhile. I was having trouble believing he had that kind of money because I'd already loaned him about $500. When I asked him about it, he had a story for me, which I swallowed hook, line and sinker like the rest of them. He said he'd been in an industrial accident back east, which had made him permanently disabled. He had filed a lawsuit, which had taken years to litigate, but eventually he'd won and was just waiting for the insurance settlement of one million dollars. He had a notarized document from the Hanford Insurance Company attesting to the amount in the final settlement. It looked legitimate. I had no reason to doubt him."

She sniffed and pressed her tissue to her nose. "I don't mind being snookered, Detective, but when I learned he was borrowing money from our church fund, with the intent to pay it back, something in my spirit warned me. Then I found out about him and Josie. Fornicating on the washers! I was shocked. I began to have real doubts."

She blew her nose and looked in her pockets for another tissue. Varland opened his side desk drawer and withdrew a tissue. He handed it to her. She smiled gratefully.

"Something else happened, didn't it, Madge; something that would provoke you to murder, a mortal sin if I'm not mistaken. What was it?"

Her face blanched. "Murder! Oh!" She looked as if she were about to faint. Varland moved the tissue box aside and pulled out a bottle of brandy. He poured a little in an empty coffee mug and came around the desk. He put it in her hand and she drank from it. She gulped, sputtered and coughed. He patted her gently on the shoulder until she stopped. He was pleased to see color return to her cheeks. He resumed his seat.

"Ugly business," he said, "isn't it, Madge? Murder. I can't see you doing it, but sometimes righteous anger leads people to do terrible things. Is that what happened?"

"Was that hard liquor?"

"Brandy," he admitted, showing her the bottle.

She blushed and more color flooded her cheeks. "I've never allowed liquor to pass my lips. It's a terrible sin."

"Almost as terrible as murder," he quipped.

"That's not funny, Detective. It's no laughing matter!"

He was glad to see her rallying again. Perhaps he would get to the bottom of her motivation. "I apologize, Madge. Go on. Finish your story. You were telling me about how Bennie was defrauding your church."

"I'm really quite annoyed with the elders. A bunch of fools, but then he took us all in, I'm sorry to say. He convinced them that in order for him to arrange for his donation, he would need some capital to set up house until his money was transferred to his bank. They gave him three thousand dollars! He

bought that awful car of his with it. When I confronted him, he laughed and told me to mind my
own business. I was shocked. I was the one who had
taken him in. I was the one who had prayed with
him and led him to the Lord. I was the one who had
introduced him to Reverend Julian, and now that
he had an in, he didn't need me any more. I guess,
well, I guess I snapped. That does happen, doesn't it,
Detective Varland?"

"I guess, sometimes. But you didn't just snap,
Madge. You appeared to have planned it. That's pre-
meditated murder."

"No, I just snapped. I saw red and I killed him."

"No, Madge, you didn't. You wanted to kill him,
but you didn't."

"I did!"

"Your story just doesn't wash, Madge. Your fingerprints are not on the washer in the laundry room.
You had no access to the wine that poisoned him.
You may have been strong once, but I can tell from
the curvature in your spine that there is no way you
could have pulled a man of Bennie's weight and size
out to the pool."

"I did kill him. You have to let Josie go. She's
innocent!" She started to cry, pressing the tissue up
to her eyes.

Varland felt suddenly tired and wretched. He hated
for the old dear to be so upset, trying desperately to

save her friend; even to admitting to a murder she didn't commit.

"Where's the croquet mallet, Madge?" he asked quietly.

"Wha-at?"

"The croquet mallet. The one you allegedly whacked him on the head with. If you can produce it, I'll arrest you for murder. Deal?"

"I . . . I threw it away."

"Come on, Madge. You've got enough sin on your soul. Don't lie anymore to me. You didn't kill him."

"No . . . I didn't kill him. I wanted to, but I didn't. I have been repenting of my evil thoughts for days. I just thought about that scripture, you know, the one Jesus said to his disciples: 'greater love has no one than to lay down his life for a friend.' When I heard Reverend Julian say those words at Bible Study, I knew they were meant for me. I'm old. I've lived a good life and have no husband or children. Josie does. I know she didn't kill Bennie. I know it! In here, Detective." She pressed her hand to her heart. Her dewy eyes pleaded with him.

"You're a good friend, Madge. I'm sure God will forgive you for lying to save her. Let me help you out to your car. You do have a car, don't you?"

"I took a taxi," she said meekly.

"I'll have an officer take you home. Come on. We won't say another word about this. If your friend is innocent, with your prayers, perhaps God will set her free."

She grimaced as she stood up, but beamed once she was up on her feet. She surprised him by giving him a bear hug. She was strong for an old woman.

"God bless you, Detective Varland. I'm going to be praying for the Lord to mightily bless you and give you the desires of your heart."

He watched as Vana took her by the elbow and escorted her down the hallway.

Imagine the courage and determination it had taken her to pull a stunt like this. He whistled and went back to his desk. He looked at his watch. It was almost three o'clock. He flipped off the overhead light, sat in his chair, swinging his legs on top of his desk and leaned back.

Now where was I?

CHAPTER TWENTY-THREE

Detective Varland's pleasant daydream had become a deep sleep until he was abruptly awakened by a firm knock on the door. He opened one eye. It was Vana. She came in and flipped on the overhead light. He swore softly and removed his feet from his desk.

"What is it, Vana?"

"Sorry, Chief, but you've got another one?"

"Another what?"

"Another old lady."

"Good grief! I haven't got time for this! Put her off. Tell her I'm out. Whatever you do, don't bring her in here. I've had all the bedtime stories I can take for one day!"

"Look, Chief, she's not just old, she's ancient. She's over ninety! I don't want her dying in the lobby. You will see her. I'm sure she won't talk long. She looks as if she's all done in."

"Oh, alright, but if I'm still with her for more than ten minutes, interrupt with an important call. Okay?"

"You got it, Chief," she said, shutting his door.

He did not recognize the woman Vana brought in. She was quite elderly but walked with sure steps, even if slowed by rheumatism. Vana brought her to the chair and indicated she should sit before she gave Varland a 'behave yourself' look and left.

The woman sat with some effort, but once settled, she looked up at him and gave him a piercing green-eyed stare. Her face was lined with deep wrinkles, but her makeup was expertly applied. Her plentiful white hair was coiffed in a becoming style. There was a touch of elegance about her. She was dressed in black slacks, a buttoned-down maroon silk blouse, and a silk jacket with glittering rhinestones sewed in starburst patterns. Her diamond necklace drew the eye away from the folds of loose skin under her chin, but the diamond teardrops hanging in her ears pulled her lobes unnaturally low. Her bony hands dazzled with several expensive rings of diamond, ruby and emerald.

"I'll get right to the point, Detective Varland. You've arrested the wrong woman. Josie Simone didn't do it. I killed Bennie Uzul," she proclaimed in a deep, throaty voice with a slight waver.

"Oh, you did, did you, ma'am? Take your time and tell me all about it."

"Are you mocking me, young man?" she demanded, leaning forward, slapping her hand on the top of his desk. Her eyes blazed with shrewd intelligence. She may be elderly, but she exuded a powerful force of vitality.

"No, ma'am," he replied, straightening up in his chair. He had a flashback of Mrs. Newman, his sixth-grade teacher, who used to whip him into shape by her rapier use of the English language.

"Good. I suggest you record what I'm about to say unless you want to interrogate me in another room."

"We can do it here." He sat back and folded his hands in front of his stomach. He smiled his beatific smile, oozing with understanding and care.

"Well, where is it?" she demanded.

"What?"

"The tape recorder. I insist!"

He frowned, disconcerted, and picked up the phone. "Vana, will you bring a tape recorder to my office. Thank you."

He hung up and gave his visitor a penetrating look. She responded with the same and he realized he was up against an entirely different kind of woman.

"Why don't you begin at the beginning," he said.

"When it's recorded, " she stated in no uncertain terms. She sat back and waited, glancing around the room with an appraising eye.

"You're a bachelor," she began, speaking almost to herself. "I'd guess fifty-five, sixty. Married to the job. No interest in settling down. You eat too much and you don't exercise. Probably like a bracer of whiskey now and again, but you're not a hard drinker. You were raised in the Upper Midwest; Minnesota would be my guess. You use the monophthongal mid vowels, which is common in Minnesota. Your parents were probably of Scandinavian extraction. It's when you said 'about' that I placed you."

Varland was stunned. He could barely speak. "I was raised in Thief River Falls, Minnesota. My parents are Norwegian-Americans. Brandy, not whiskey."

"Brandy, eh? Darn. My nose isn't what it used to be. Getting old, I guess."

"I guess not! That was amazing! Who are you, Sherlock Holmes?"

She laughed a laugh that reminded him of Lauren Bacall. "You should have seen me in the day, young man, or should I call you by your title, Chief of Detectives Magnus Varland."

He grinned. "Detective Varland is fine."

At that moment, Vana came in and placed a small black rectangle on his desk.

"What is this?" he asked.

"It's a voice activated digital recorder."

"What's wrong with the one we had where you put a tape in it?"

Vana scowled at him. "Look. All you do is turn it on. Even you can do that, sir."

"Then how will you transcribe it if there's no tape? Are you sure about this?"

He heard the old woman chuckling under her breath. He felt like a dinosaur and flushed up to his sandy roots.

"Don't worry about that, sir. I just connect it to my computer. Trust me."

"Very well."

"Uhm, about that important phone call you're waiting for. Still want me to send it through?"

"Take a message. Thank you, Vana. You may go."

As soon as she shut the door, he turned on the recorder and pushed it to the end of the desk. He looked at his watch.

"It is 2:15 p.m., August 29th. Chief of Detectives Magnus Varland interviewing. Please state your name and address for the record, ma'am."

"Dorthea Blum. My friends call me Diddi. I live at 3560 Superstition Way, Unit #1600, Peralto Canyon, Arizona. I'm here to confess that I murdered Bennie Uzul, but I'll tell you right now, Detective Varland, I'll never see the inside of a courtroom. I have an inoperable brain tumor. My number's up, so to speak. I'll croak any day now."

He was startled and sorry to hear her say that. He liked her. Just like all the old dears, he couldn't help himself. For her sake, he was willing to continue the charade. He knew he had the right woman in custody. This was just another one of Josie Simone's misguided friends who wanted to save her.

"Please start from the beginning, Ms. Blum."

"It began a long, long time ago, Detective Varland, probably when you were just a child. If I have to, I'll go into that, but suffice it to say that it was only recently that I planned Bennie Uzul's murder. I have a close friend, perhaps you know her: Maddie Ingersoll."

"Oh yes, I know, Mrs. Ingersoll. Lovely woman."

"She's a bit dotty, but she has the sweetest soul on the planet. She's 85, but the years have not made her turn bitter or suspicious. Not like me. She's loving and good, always trying to help people, and never thinking bad about them. Unlike me. I love her as if she were my own little sister. She came to me about a month ago and asked my advice. One of her 'strays' needed her help. His name was Bennie Uzul. She wanted to know if she should lend him money to buy a car. She told me all this baloney that the guy was using to persuade her. I told her that I couldn't advise her until I'd met the guy. We arranged for me to just show up when he was there.

"He was a smooth talker, I'll give him that. Unfortunately for him, he thought I was just another naive, doddering old woman, and tried to put the touch on me, too. I let him weave his tale of woe. It was pretty convincing; too convincing. I was beginning to grow even more suspicious of him. It wasn't until I said goodbye and shook his hand that I got the shock of my life and began to plot his demise."

"What was it about the handshake that tipped you off, Ms. Blum?"

"I'll get to that," she said, frowning at being

interrupted. She searched her mind, wiping her bejeweled hand across her brow until she remembered. "I pretty much figured from the first that I would poison him. I just needed an opportunity. I began following him, learning his habits, taking notes. I used to be able to keep it all in my head, but now, with the brain tumor and all I find I have to write things down. I brought my notes if you want them."

He nodded. Satisfied, she continued: "I found out pretty quick about Josie. It was a bit of a shock, but back in the day, I had a tryst or two in unusual places."

He watched as her face softened by a sweet memory, and then hardened as if the memory pained her.

She cleared her throat. "They regularly met at 4 a.m. in the Laundromat, every Wednesday. He always got there first. He waited until the security patrol passed and then went in—our Laundromat is open 24/7, Detective, so any resident can use it at any time. Josie came in about 4:05. He put coins in two washing machines and while the machines went through their cycle, he and Josie engaged in foreplay. When the machines reached the spin cycle, they stripped and climbed up on the lids. That's where they had sex—on the washing machine lids during the spin cycle. Pretty inventive, I thought. I'd wish I'd tried it—back in the day." She smiled shyly up at Varland and he felt himself blushing.

"Go on," he said in a strangled voice. "What did you do then?"

"It was the same every time. After Josie left, Bennie would do yoga stretches and then go into the ante-room, bare-assed naked, sit on the couch and smoke a couple cigarettes. He was always careful. Before he'd sit on the couch he'd get some paper towels from the men's room and place them on the couch to sit on. Before Security came around again, he'd put on his clothes, stuff the butts in his pocket and then wipe down everything he had touched. After that, he'd get into his car and leave. Too bad for him he was a creature of habit. I learned his routine fairly quickly."

"You amaze me, Ms. Blum!" Detective Varland gushed, sitting back and wagging his head.

"Call me Diddi. Ms. Blum only reminds me that I never married."

"Oh. I can't believe it. I'm sure you were quite a catch—back in the day."

She smiled. "Thank you. I was. Back to my confession. It was really just a matter of opportunity. I had decided on strychnine early on. It is a horrible way to die. It switches off the nerve signals to the muscles throughout the body, eventually causing horrific painful spasms. It's agony. The muscles spasm, the back arches and the face contorts. The person is conscious the whole time until the muscles tire and they can't breathe, causing death.

"You wanted him to suffer," Varland breathed out, riveted by her casual description of the mode of Bennie's death.

"Oh yes, the more painful, the better. I particularly liked that he was fully conscious and knew that it was me who had poisoned him. That's why I settled on strychnine. My only roadblock was finding a means of administering it. I gave that quite a lot of thought. Strychnine is odorless, but it has a pretty nasty taste. I needed something strong to mask it, something that he would drink willingly. Speaking of drinking, you wouldn't by any chance have any of your brandy handy. I haven't talked this much in years."

Varland quickly pulled out his brandy and looked around for a clean cup. He found a commemorative wine glass from last year's Christmas party and splashed a finger of brandy into it. He handed it to her, which she accepted gratefully. Riveted by her story, he quickly returned to his seat. He watched as she sipped on it, clearing her throat.

"That's good. Just the ticket," she said, tossing the rest down. She caught her breath and breathed out fumes. "Ahh. Well, it wasn't until I was at Boom Boom's house with Maddie that the means became clear. Maddie had made curtains for Boom Boom's bedroom and I tagged along. I think you've met Boom Boom, isn't that right, Detective? I see by your grin

that you have. She's a fanatic about wine. I prefer
white and she loves red, Merlot as a matter of fact.
She was quite proud that she had stocked her wine
cabinet with one bottle of Chardonnay for me—isn't
that thoughtful of her—and a case of Merlot for her.
She had so many bottles and she's a bit of a scatter-
brain, so I knew she wouldn't miss it. I lifted a bottle
and hid it in my car while she and Maddie were going
on about the curtains. Now I had means. I just needed
to wait for the right opportunity."

She held out her glass and he quickly splashed in
some more brandy. She took a sip and held the glass
by the stem, twirling it before she continued.

"You see, my original plan, Detective Varland,
was to string him along as one of his pigeons and
then strike, but then Maddie told me she was planning to give him $20,000 so he could go into busi-
ness for himself—a plane service for the locals. What
hogwash! Well, Detective Varland, I wasn't going to
let him rob my friend of twenty thou. I had to put my
plan into action immediately.

"Like I told you, I knew his habits pretty well. He
liked to go to the pool around two and sit in the spa.
I made sure I was already there. It was pretty easy
to hook him. I told him how I had all this money
and was looking for a worthy cause. He gave me
the same song and dance about his plane service.
I acted like I was eager to become his partner and

told him I could give him a check for $50,000. He bit like a spawning salmon. I arranged for us to meet at 4:30 a.m. Wednesday morning. I knew he'd be there hooking up with Josie. He readily agreed.

"That morning, after Josie left, I came in with my basket of tricks. He had the decency, you might say, to have on his boxer shorts, but he was pretty high on himself right then and said, 'Won't you join me in my office, partner?' What a buffoon. I followed him into the anteroom off the main laundry. We sat on the couch together. I gave him a check for $50,000. I could see the greed oozing from his eyes. The time was ripe. I needed to keep him there and set the stage. I offered him a couple croissants and some Gouda, just to keep him off guard. We ate and talked about our new business venture. He was in rare form, boasting and concocting lie after lie. That's when I pulled out the bottle of Merlot from my basket.

"'Let's toast to our partnership,' I said. He was pleased as punch, commenting on my good taste in wine. I allowed him to uncork it, while I pulled two plastic cups from my basket. While he was messing with uncorking the wine, I laced one cup with strychnine, enough to kill him within five to ten minutes. He was so elated with his triumph that he didn't even notice the liquid in the bottom. I held the cups and he poured the wine.

"'To our new partnership,' he said and downed

the wine. He made a face and I was afraid he might catch on, but he didn't. He poured himself another cupful and drank that as well.

"It was then that I said to him, 'You don't remember me, do you? But I remember you, Borysko Orlyk!'

"He jumped up and looked like a rat caught in a trap. 'Who are you?' His eyes literally bulged out of his skull. I loved seeing the terror in his eyes as he tried to place me.

"'I've killed you, Borysko,' I said, taunting him, looking him straight in the eyes. At that moment, he knew the truth. 'You're a traitor, Borysko, I said, and you deserve a traitor's death! For Michael Coughlin. Remember him? You murdered him, you piece of filth, and I have avenged him this day!'"

She took a gulp of brandy. He noticed her breathing was becoming more labored. Before she could go on, he interrupted her, "Forgive me, I've heard that name before. Michael Coughlin. Who is he?"

She smiled wistfully. "The only man I ever loved. He was a CIA operative during the Cold War, stationed in Berlin."

"That's it!" Varland exclaimed, slapping his forehead. "That's where I heard his name. Bennie was a spy for the CIA. I didn't believe it, but it's true. I saw the identification numbers between his fingers."

"Like these?" she asked, stretching her bony bejeweled fingers out to him. He came around the desk and took her hand. She spread her fingers apart and he could just make out the faded numbers tattooed in the webbing. Varland was dumbfounded. He went back to his chair and fell into it, rubbing his head.

"That means that . . . you're a . . . "

"Spy, too? Yes, Detective Varland. I was also in Berlin and Michael Coughlin was my lover. I always suspected Borysko was behind his death, but I couldn't prove it, and then he disappeared. I searched for him for years. I learned he had been spotted in the Phoenix area, so I moved here ten years ago. Imagine my shock when I shook his hand and saw the numbers between his fingers."

"That's when you decided to kill him," Varland surmised.

"Oh no. I've planned to kill him since 1980. I knew he was the traitor. I had no proof and no one would listen to me. Bennie was a valuable asset at the time. But, I knew. I vowed someday to avenge my dear Michael and his partner, John Priestly. I had no idea it was going to take me nearly forty years before I could. Shall I go on?"

Varland nodded his head and took a sip of brandy from the bottle.

"Well, after I poisoned him, I was so caught up in my triumph seeing him grovel at my feet that I didn't realize he'd dropped to the floor for a reason. He had reached under the couch for a weapon. Too bad for him that the poison was already at work. His arms jerked and he lost control of his fingers. The weapon dropped to the floor and I kicked it out of his reach. He grabbed for me, but I easily stepped out of his way. I believe I laughed at him and told him he was going to die any minute.

"He fled and goose-stepped past me and out the door. I picked up the weapon and followed him, watching him jerk and twitch, trying to cry out, but only gurgling, grabbing at his throat. I followed him all the way to the lower pool. He couldn't get away from me. I savored every moment. I had waited a long time for this."

She stopped and sipped on her brandy. To Varland's horror, she smiled at the recollection. She looked up and saw his expression. She shrugged her shoulders. "He was an evil man, Detective Varland, and deserved to die. He was a cancer that had to be eradicated. He was a traitor to his country and murdered my Michael, a good and decent patriot who was trying to help someone escape the tyranny of Communism. I don't expect you to understand. It was a different time. My actions are justified."

She opened her purse and pulled out a vial of a colorless liquid.

"Here, Detective Varland, is the murder weapon."

He pulled a tissue from the drawer and picked

it up, careful not to leave any prints. He saw her watching him and he felt foolish. "What did you do then?" Varland queried, trying to keep his cool.

"I watched him die," she said simply, "poolside. He fell to the ground, his back arched and his arms convulsed, then he lay still."

"And the weapon he was going to use on you?" Varland asked, leaning forward.

"The croquet mallet? It's in my car." She grimaced. "I put it to good use. His head was the ball and I gave it a good whack. I was actually trying to knock him into the pool; unfortunately, it wasn't entirely successful, so I had to use my foot to kick him the rest of the way in. I just sort of shoved him over the edge, like the piece of trash he was. I would have stayed there and waited for the police if it hadn't been for Alice."

"Alice?"

"Alice Sheridan. You remember. She found the body, poor dear. I feel bad about that. I had no idea she would show up at the moment of my triumph. I'm embarrassed to say I panicked and ran. Even cold-blooded murderers have a soft spot for the elderly. So! There you have it. That's my confession. Are you going to release Josie now?"

Chapter Twenty-Four

The morning was cool. The temperature had dropped to a pleasant eighty degrees. The sky was bright blue—achingly blue. The regal long palms swayed to a gentle rhythm produced by a whimsical breeze. A thrush sang a spritely tune as the ladies of the Superstition Aquatics Club came to pay their respects to their old friend.

They walked arm and arm, in pairs and in threes, to the gravesite. After a valiant fight, their friend Dorthea "Diddi" Blum was laid to rest. The service was short and sweet, as she had requested.

Only two passages were read: Emily Dickinson's "Wild Nights!" which Boom Boom Klutterbuck read and Mary Elizabeth Frye's "Do Not Stand By My Grave and Weep," read by Maddie Ingersoll. Cicie Kimbro sang "Amazing Grace" between scripture readings recited by Madge Ziegler and Loretta Dukes.

"It was lovely. Wasn't it lovely?" Veronica wept as they walked back to their cars. This was the first funeral she had attended since she had made Arizona her home and it brought into focus the precious and fleeting time she would have with the ladies of the Superstition Aquatics Club.

Sweets put her arm around her shoulders and gave her a squeeze. "Classy, just like Diddi."

"All this time and I never knew," Babe Winters mourned, leaning heavily on Bella Adler. "She never told me. She knew my John. All this time and I never knew."

"She was deep," Bella agreed. "I will miss her so much."

"She was a pioneer; one of the greats!" Sandra declared with gusto to Cicie and Maddie as she linked arms with them and helped them over the last rise to the street. "Did you know she was one of the first female officers in the CIA who received a Grade-14? She worked under Truman, Eisenhower, Kennedy and Johnson. What a role model! I wish I'd known, boy, what a story I could have written."

"She was always so secretive about her past," Maddie cried. "I thought she was just being polite because I talked so much. Now I know why. She was a spy. Did you know that?"

"Yes, we know, Maddie," Cicie said, patting her friend's hand.

"I'm really going to miss her. Who's going to keep me straight now?"

"We all will, Maddie," Loretta said, striding up beside them.

"She always said exactly what she thought and she only said something when it was necessary," Cicie inserted. "I'm going to try to be more like her."

"Yes, a woman of great intelligence who knew how to say a lot with just a few words," Bella agreed.

"There are no words," Josie lamented, her cheeks wet with tears. "No words. She saved my life."

"And mine," Madge nodded, sagely. "I was so sure God told me to confess to set you free."

"I know. I'm very grateful, Madge," Josie smiled. "You're a true friend."

"And mine and John's," Sandra interrupted. "I'm sure after they let you go, Josie, they were going to arrest us next. It was John's croquet mallet, did you hear?"

"Only about a million times," Boom Boom wailed, punching Sandra in the arm. "Don't forget it was my wine! My own Merlot! Kissy-poo and I were shocked. I'm drinking Cabernet from now on."

"Did John get his mallet back? I understand it was custom made," Madge asked.

"It's still in the evidence room. I have to ask Detective Varland when he can release it. I'm not sure John will want it back, knowing what it was used for. It cost me a lot of money."

Chief of Detectives Magnus Varland stood apart from the group who mourned Diddi Blum. He wanted to be there, to pay homage to the woman who had avenged her lover and her country, but he wasn't sure his presence would be welcomed. He had imposed himself on the small band of women enough: he had intruded on their well-ordered lives, interrogated them, and even arrested two of them.

They had taught him more about life than he had realized. His prejudice against older women had blinded him to their intelligence, tenacity and loyalty. He should have listened to them more and trusted their instincts and possibly saved them from his blundering arrogance.

"You seem far away," Petey's voice filtered through his thoughts of recrimination.

Her sudden nearness startled him. He hadn't even realized she had moved away from the group and joined him.

"Thinking about Diddi," he said.

She put her arm through his and hugged it.

"Gives you a new appreciation for the elderly, doesn't it?" she said softly, speaking his thoughts. "We forget that we're just like them. Even if our bodies get old, we're still the same on the inside. Imagine being ninety-five and seeing the man who stole your life, the man who had killed the only man you ever loved. Imagine seeing him walking around, enjoying life while he had destroyed others, and knowing he was still doing it."

"I know what you mean. I was thinking the same." He gave her arm a squeeze by pressing it closer to his body. "I can't get over how calmly and confidently she confessed to a brutal murder."

"He was an evil man," she reminded him, speaking Diddi's words, "and she was a trained operative, but I admit I am conflicted about what she did."

"So am I," he admitted, watching the ladies from the Superstition Aquatics Club move away from the gravesite. They were helping each other walk over the rise, comforting one another, giving each other support in their grief. He turned, breaking away from her grip, and looked her in the eyes. "I am a sworn officer of the law, Petey. I had to arrest her."

She looked startled at the vehemence of his words. She smiled sadly and took his hand. "She expected nothing less, Magnus."

"Then why do I feel like the traitor, like I'm as low as Bennie Uzul?"

"Don't say that!" she pulled on his hand. "You are a good man! Diddi was wrong to take the law into her own hands. She was wrong to set herself up as judge, jury and executioner, even for someone as loathsome as Bennie Uzul. She knew it when she did it and I will be forever grateful. That man killed my father, Magus; a father I never got to know except through my mother's recollections and she rarely talked about him. One of the reasons I joined the Company was so I could find out more about him, to be near him, in a way."

He heard the catch in her throat and his arms ached to pull her into him, to comfort her, to share his strength with her. Instead, he squeezed her fingers.

"I know. She was one of a kind and I'm glad I got to be in her life, even if it was for only a short time in terrible circumstances. She was right, you know. She never saw the inside of a jail cell or a courtroom."

"I visited her in the hospital just a few days before she died. I wasn't sure she would be aware of me, but I had to go and thank her personally. Do you know what she said to me?"

"With Diddi, I can't even imagine."

"She said I looked like my father. She told me things about him that I never knew. She told me . . ." she choked and wiped her eyes.

Magnus put his arm around her shoulders and hugged her close.

"She told me that the night I was born he was with John Coughlin in Berlin. They got roaring drunk celebrating and he spent the night in a torrential downpour chiseling my name on the Berlin Wall. When John asked him why he was doing that, he said, 'because I want her to be here when they bring this damn wall down.'"

"That's a good story," Magnus smiled, giving her shoulders a little shake before letting her go. "That's a story a daughter should know about her father."

"Yes," she said, wiping her eyes and giving him

her dazzling smile. "Isn't it? Do you know what her code name was?"

"I have no idea. Cobra? Avenger? Terminator?"

She smiled, showing her beautiful teeth. "No. Pretty Baby." She laughed.

"Wow. That's deep cover. What's your code name, Petey?"

"I don't have one."

"Right. If you told me would you have to kill me?"

"I might."

"Do you have to take your mother back home?" he asked.

"She's going with her friends. They're headed for Diddi's favorite watering hole. Maddie's hired a limo for the whole afternoon. I guess I'm free."

"Would you like to go to my favorite watering hole?"

"Yes, Magnus, I would."

He took her arm and guided her to his car.

Meanwhile, the ladies from the Aquatics Club gathered at the stretch limousine and made plans.

"You can leave your car in the parking lot, Josie, and come with us. The driver will bring you back here," Mimi said with agreement from the others.

"I don't know. David wants me home."

"He can't expect you to just come home after Diddi's funeral. Call him!" Sandra demanded. "John already knows not to expect me. Tell him that if it weren't for Diddi, he'd be visiting you in jail!"

"Oh, Miss-Behavin', you have done it again!" Mimi laughed. "Foot in mouth syndrome can be cured, you know."

"I'm not leaving my bike," Sweets argued. "I'll meet you all there."

"Where's Babe?"

"She and Bella left already. They'll meet us there," Loretta informed them.

"Did anyone see Detective Varland. Was he here?" Maddie asked. "Such a nice man. I made him a pillow."

"I saw him," Margarita gloated, coming up to the limo, arm and arm with her new boyfriend, Bay. "He's here and you'll never guess who he's with?"

"Who?" Sandra wanted to know.

"Guess!" Margarita urged.

"Oh, I don't know! Detective Rinaldi?" Sweets replied.

"No."

"That nice woman, what's-her-name?" Veronica guessed.

"Vana?" Cicie suggested.

"No! Babe's daughter, Petey!"

"Special Agent Winters?" Boom Boom laughed. "Wait 'til I tell Kissy-poo!"

"Is something going on there?" Veronica asked.

"You can ask Babe in the morning," Sandra inserted. "Our hiatus is over, my friends. She expects us to be in the pool by seven sharp! The Superstition Aquatics Club lives to swim another day!"

What's next for the ladies of The Superstition Murder Club?

Too Soon For Sunset

Watch for it!